TONE SCHUNNESSON (Malmö, 1988) is a Swedish writer. She studied Creative Writing and debuted in 2016 with *Trip Reports*, which received critical acclaim and was shortlisted for the Borås Tidning's Debutant Prize. Her first non-fiction book, *Tone: Round-Trip Ticket* (2022), is a collection of political gonzo essays. *Days & Days & Days* is her second novel. It was shortlisted for the EU Prize for Literature 2021 and Sveriges Radio's Novel Prize for Best Swedish Novel 2021.

SASKIA VOGEL was born and raised in Los Angeles and now lives in its sister city, Berlin, where she works as a writer, screenwriter, and translator from Swedish and German into English. In 2021 she was awarded the Berlin Senate grant for non-German literature, two English PEN Translates Awards, and was a PEN America Translation Prize finalist. She was Princeton's Fall 2022 Translator in Residence.

Tone Schunnesson

DAYS & DAYS & DAYS

TRANSLATED FROM THE SWEDISH
BY SASKIA VOGEL

HÉ/OÏSE

PRESS

First published in English in Great Britain in 2023 by
Héloïse Press Ltd
4 Pretoria Road
Canterbury CT1 1QL

www.heloisepress.com

Dagarna, dagarna, dagarna © Tone Schunnesson, first published by
Norstedts, Sweden, in 2020

Published by agreement with Norstedts Agency

This translation © Saskia Vogel 2023

Cover design by Laura Kloos
Edited by Nichola Smalley
Text design and typesetting by Tetragon, London
Printed and bound in Great Britain by CPI Group (UK) Ltd, Croydon, CR0 4YY

The cost of this translation was supported by a subsidy from the Swedish Arts Council, gratefully acknowledged.

ISBN 978-1-7397515-6-2

DAYS
& DAYS &
DAYS

When I walked into my medium's office, the summer after my first reality TV show became a hit, she told me that I looked different. 'Skinny?' I asked, full of hope, and Marite replied: 'No, established.' For three years I'd sent her ten grand every twelve weeks for unlimited access to her in-person services, plus phone calls, if I called after four. 'You're lost in the sauce,' was one of the last things she said to me, years later, when the knuckles on my right hand were raw after punching the door to our building on Slipgatan. Baby was supposed to come with me to some whisky event when out of nowhere he decided it was bullshit. The static started one street down from our apartment, shortly after the homeless woman I'd see around Reimersholme Island sailed towards us like a wraith. 'Could you spare a cigarette?' she asked. I tightened my fist around the pack and turned away from her. 'I can pay,' she said. OK, so that'll be 200SEK, then, I said, avoiding eye contact, eager to keep fighting – the fight was the only thing that could get my Baby to stay. Baby said, 'For Christ's sake, Bibbs. Give her a cigarette,' and without thinking I turned around and threw the pack in her face. Baby looked at me and said you fucking psycho bitch. The cigarettes tumbled onto the wet asphalt. Come morning the leaves on the trees would all be gone, and the bleak state that would reign for months would take hold within hours. Baby entered the code that unlocked the building's door and when it slammed shut in my face, with Baby on the other side, I punched it. It took a moment for my hand to start bleeding, slowly, as if the wound were hesitating. Got a light? the woman asked, and I rooted around in my bag, knuckles burning. I imagined that I'd punched the door in rage, but really it was a bid to reconnect with myself. Yes, I was getting lost in the sauce, I can't explain it any better than that. I'd have preferred to have greater strength of character. Wouldn't we all. Everyone whose character is weak has at some point fantasised about it being strong.

My time with Marite changed me, but I stopped visiting her in Årsta after she told me that I'd got lost in the sauce and because she was sinking all of her income, savings too, into building an app that no one would ever pay for. The app let you shoot videos in slow motion. Marite wore amber necklaces, and when she told me about the idea I didn't want to hurt her feelings, so I didn't let slip that everyone could already do this. Everyone but Marite, with her burner phone and solo fiftieth birthday bash in Peru. After the app launched, she started calling me more often than I was calling her, and with rising desperation. She owed her team in Poland a lot of money, and instead of paying what she owed she'd assign new tasks each week. The bills were piling up. 'Bibbs,' she said when she called, hoping to sell me more hours, 'there's no such thing as investing too much in your health.' Hold on a second, how did you find those people in Poland, I wanted to know, and she told me that a window had popped up while googling, so she typed in it. Got it, I said, but I was out of money. Maybe you could promote the app? she'd ask me more than once during each phone call. I didn't want to promote the app. The app would align me with failure in far too obvious a way.

My visits to Marite were something I'd afforded myself in a year when the money was basically rolling in on its own. Then my lucky streak ran out, and Marite ended up being yet another expense among others when she started seeing me with a clarity I could live without. I started only taking her calls sometimes and stopped calling without telling her why. How could I tell her that I'd been shooting slow-motion videos for years and that her feeling bad was only making me feel worse? Not to mention, I couldn't afford her. I didn't have the heart to say that everything had seemed so brilliant, until it didn't anymore.

I will never forgive myself for not realising that Baby was preparing to leave me. Looking back I can see the signs, but they were hard to interpret before I knew what I know now. He'd been unusually critical of me while I was packing for one of my work trips but I didn't care, as I so often didn't care about him.

'So, you're off on some glorified bar tour, like a bona fide reality TV star.'

Not really paying attention, I'd defended myself. It wasn't a bar tour. Who even goes on bar tours anymore? It was a performance that happened to be in a bar, and I was going to be interviewed about linear television.

'Is it just you?'

'Dunno.' But it wasn't just me. It was a former Eurodisco singer, the man who introduced 'bouncer's choice' to Swedish club culture, and a porn star who'd turned fifty.

'And some art school student is organising it?'

'No, not a student, well, it's his final degree project.'

'Don't say "degree", Bibbs, as if getting wasted with has-beens is some sort of science.'

'My bad.' Baby didn't have a degree and hadn't gone to university, but each month he was paid the same salary at the same time, even if he'd been sick. This gave him an authority that was hard for me to touch.

My invoice would be for ten grand, because the student was collaborating with a credit score service. Travel and accommodation were taken care of. The appearance would happen at a bar in Gothenburg, and I'd be staying at Hôtel Eggers, a grand old hotel appointed with blue heavyweight fabric and period cabinetry. When we visited Gothenburg, Baby loved staying at the Eggers. Maybe this was why he was sulking, I'd thought. He hated it when I went away and liked to pick fights with me beforehand so I wouldn't be able to leave him behind, not really. I'd carry him around like a manic thought, even after I arrived at my destination. Baby loved staying in hotels, but hated paying for them. I'd gladly foot the bill if it made him happy, but because I was the one who usually covered this expense we hadn't been able to in a while.

I always packed several wardrobe changes because my outfit was always a comment on what I was doing, whatever I was doing. Before Baby came home from work I'd put on my everyday face and change into my at-home clothes; one of the things that had first attracted me to Baby was how considered his clothing was. A couple of years into the relationship he started wearing sweatpants around the house, and I teased him until he stopped. In spite of his comparatively low income his wardrobe included expensive turtlenecks and limited-edition shoes. Baby took good – too good – care of his clothes which meant that in the winter he'd point out every ladder in my stockings, and get his kicks de-pilling his coats in the evenings. Most of the expensive items in my closet had been sent to me and so I wasn't particularly attached to them; I'm not sure I'd have bought them in the first place, like I wasn't sure if (had it been a choice) I'd have used the moisturisers on my shelf or got the haircut my hairdresser gave me in exchange for photos. Baby would follow me around like an anxious maid, snatching dresses off the wet bathroom floor and hanging them up properly. 'Four thousand,' he'd say. 'This is 4,000 kronor right here.'

A week ago on Saturday I returned home from the glorified bar tour, giving no thought to Baby's objection to the gig. I felt light and happy. I'd basked in the attention in Gothenburg and had stayed away from carbs for two days. When I came into the bedroom, Baby was sitting on the bed, back straight, and wearing a long-sleeved white T-shirt and a pair of mid-thigh shorts by Thom Browne, which I'd bought him the summer we stayed at Soho House in Berlin. Before I had a chance to kiss him, he said: I'm leaving you.

This leaving came as a surprise. I'm still surprised. I never thought he'd have the guts, plus he wanted a quick exit, no drama. I could tell our days were numbered by his conversational tone. This time the leaving was different to how I'd usually leave him, wound-up and loud, like the denouement of an argument. I'd hear him behind me, begging me to stay, as I slammed the door in a rage.

'The moment has arrived, Bibbs.' For the first time in ages I noticed that I liked the look of him. Those long limbs and a gold hoop in one ear. How often had we left each other, in hysterics? OK, so he wasn't usually the one who'd walk out of the apartment, but leaving takes countless forms. The time I cut up his good shirt right in front of him and he slapped the scissors out of my hand and their tip scratched me, hadn't he left me then? But in a situation like that it's impossible for either party to actually walk out. Or what about the time the police stopped us on the street and asked how thing were going here then after I'd hurled my key ring at him – we'd clung to each other, loyal to the end. But now Baby was saying the moment had arrived. I was standing in front of him, unsure of what to do. I'd just been considering taking a nap on the bed, which wouldn't be appropriate now. Out of habit I started doing sums in my head, like I did sums when-ever I was faced with a large expense. I couldn't afford to be left. Baby's thighs looked yellowish tan in those white shorts. The muscle above his knee tensing and relaxing was appeal-ing. Neither could I afford to admit to Baby that I couldn't afford to be left. 'Give me one good reason why you have to leave,' I said, instead of stretching out on the bed. 'One single reason.'

We don't have any mutual interests
   (But you don't even have interests)
   You don't do anything all day
   (And this bothers you why, you're at work anyway)

You lie about everything
(No, I don't)
Our fights are too violent
(I thought you liked that)
You don't want to have children with me
(But I don't want to have children with ANYONE)

Baby rubbed his face with his hands, which he thought were disproportionately small. He was clean-shaven, as he was on every special occasion. He had a hand complex. But he thought he was great at oral sex. He wasn't, and I kept that to myself, to compensate for, or to balance out, the hand thing. When we first met he would tell me stories about the women he'd gone down on, how much they'd enjoyed it. Sometimes when I walked around at home and entered the meditative state that comes with performing repetitive everyday tasks I'd catch myself thinking about those women, wondering about the noises they'd made. The images I had of Baby with other women were as potent as the image of Baby coming inside me.

'OK, Bibbs, so maybe I don't have a good reason other than not wanting to take care of you anymore.'

I felt myself harden and sensed the opening for a discussion was closing. I wanted to grab my bag, get out of there, and restage my arrival. Restage my trip. Restage whatever it was that had pushed Baby over the edge. The pleasure I was taking in his appearance vanished. The landscape we were standing in was barren.

'You can't say that to me,' I said.

'I know, you don't want to hear it. But that's how it is. There you go. I don't have it in me anymore.'

How could I have been so stupid as not to understand that his help was conditional? Was this some form of, well, I don't know. Oppression? I'd kept explaining to him that things would turn around soon, I'd turn myself around soon. I was actually easier to live with than I'd made myself out to be.

'I'm going to be raking it in again in no time.'

'Dammit Bibbs, this isn't about the money.'

Of course it was about the money. Everything was about the money, between friends or ex-lovers. Trying to buy time, I started searching the wardrobe for a crisp white shirt, my back to him. There is no retort to the money, no answer as good as that one. Behind me I heard Baby leave the bed, where he'd been sitting since my return.

'Where are you going?' I asked.

'What do you mean?'

'I thought you were leaving.'

In a voice that belonged to another time, a loving, loving time, Baby said:

'No. I'm not going anywhere.'

I heard him sit back down, but I didn't want to turn around. If I did, he'd catch something in my face that I didn't want to reveal.

'It's not about the money. You haven't had money for years, Bibbs.'

'Sure, but I do have some stashed away.'

I'd been maintaining this lie ever since we'd got to know each other four years ago, in order to make clear to Baby that I was an independent creature and could go where I wanted when I wanted. Unfortunately no one had actually saved any money for me, something I'd bring up with my mother after a few glasses of wine, to which she'd say: 'You're middle-aged, Bibbs, you're supposed to do your own saving.' But I'd always hated starting at zero, no matter what. Unlike me, Baby thought it was silly to maintain the lie but he didn't have the language with which to confront it. So we let it sit there between us, like a half-truth. The first time I uttered the lie, several years ago, it hadn't been a lie. It had been an intention. I was going to start saving any day now, I thought, and then the lie would dissolve into the truth. Any mention of these savings would make us uncomfortable, and we couldn't bring ourselves to broach the subject. Like, couldn't he have just helped me out, I'd think? He could've said I know you don't have any money, or started saving for me. On certain days I thought: 'Bibbs, if only you'd started saving the first time it occurred to you you'd be rolling in it by now.'

'OK, so since you have savings, isn't it a little odd that you haven't dipped into them this entire spring, and left me to pay for almost all of our fixed expenses myself?'

True. Baby had taken care of the rent. But I had selected every single piece of furniture and artwork in the apartment myself, because before I met him I'd shut my eyes every night and fantasize about myself so hard it made my whole face tense. When it was time to realise my fantasy, I knew exactly what to do. The art deco mirror in the hall. The velvet sofa.

Marble coasters, the silver tray, which we would do coke off one night when we returned from a lavish wedding and wanted to keep being awake, keep on talking, no, *conversing*, with each other, aroused, curious. I did up the interiors exactly as they were in my imagination, and sometimes when I took a break from scrolling through porn on the sofa and looked around the room, at the decor, I wondered if there wasn't an important distinction between fantasy and desire after all. You don't *have* to do everything you fantasise about.

The glass coffee table on which the silver tray was placed, the table I'd had to buy twice because Baby had stumbled over the first one, shattering it into a thousand pieces. Blood mixed with the glass mixed with his confused drunken words. Did I leave him then? No, I didn't leave him any of those times, and that was how I paid my share of the rent. The smudge stick, which was by the window, was my idea too, and I'd light that sage whenever I wanted to drive out a stubborn hangover. After the night of the table I also bought incense, which I stuck in the cactus that had cost a pretty penny.

Now Baby was leaning against the door frame, looking into the bedroom, which I had done up like a hotel room. I sat down in the lambswool-clad chair. We were both silent, which diverged from our usual leaving protocol. That face I'd observed so many times. Had I ever met another man with the same self-annihilating vanity? No, impossible. I choked up. How many hours had I spent looking at him while we sat across from each other on a train or on all those nights when he was asleep but I was awake. My sleeplessness had never bothered Baby, which hurt me but he said it shouldn't. His throat was red and blotchy where he'd been rubbing it. Stress and alcohol would do that to him. Had he been drinking. Maybe I shouldn't care.

Baby would say that I was careless with money but when we moved in together I got into a mode of working hard and handling my expenses accordingly. Every morning I refreshed the auction sites to see what had come in during the night and I comparison-shopped if I was going to buy something new. I bought the sofa interest-free (for the first year) on Baby's credit card, because by then my three credit cards were already maxed out. Not to mention, I had decorated each room for erotics. Naively so, because Baby would never fuck me in the kitchen. Baby could only spontaneously fuck back when we were still strangers to each other; he still fucked like he was someone else, and I was just another female vessel, filled with what he wanted me to be filled with. That's when he could allow his fantasy to mingle with his desire; my desire posed no threat to his idealisation of me.

After living here together for a while our sexuality went missing. 'Come up, come up,' he'd said, stressing out in the darkness as I sucked him off. What, was it bad? I asked. I don't like that clucking sound, it feels disrespectful, he replied and fended off my kiss with a friendly peck. Obviously his impotence bored me, but his pathological Madonna–whore complex did make me feel like the most important person in the world. I was his good little wife. Who knows where he got that insane idea from, but it amused me.

'We're not even sleeping together,' Baby said.

'You're the one who doesn't want to.'

Baby said it doesn't matter who wants to and who doesn't.

'But we slept together the other week,' I said. 'We can do it again right now,' I pleaded.

The bedroom had heard this discussion many times.

'I'll help you out until you're on your feet,' Baby said instead of approaching me with hot hands, 'and you can live here until you find something else.'

This was almost more incomprehensible than him leaving.

'What do you mean "until I find something else"? Isn't this my apartment?'

The upstairs neighbour slammed his door so hard it rattled our bedroom walls, and we heard him shout to someone that he was home. We had no idea where he'd been. Baby smoothed his hand over his head, a habit from when he still had hair. He was five years older than me. That thick hair of his was a living legend; tales were told so that it would never be forgotten, and Baby had shown me many pictures from when it still existed. What if this was the last I'd ever see of him. I reached for him, then changed my mind.

'Beautiful men and ugly women,' this is how I started my speech back on his fortieth birthday, and Baby had laughed, along with his friends. So I guess I really was ugly, I thought, because their laughter was saying that it was funny because it was true. Of course Baby's friends had known who I was and because many of them didn't live in Stockholm I was the only person they knew who was on television. One had seen me on the cover of a girlfriend's magazine but I'd looked so different then, he said, he could hardly recognise me.

Baby's face was wonderful, even if with time I'd tired of the beauty that made it possible for him to smugly remind me that he hadn't been unfaithful. 'This is the first time I've been faithful,' he'd said again and again, a threat masquerading as a compliment. His largess was forever hanging over me, which meant that I never permitted myself to put on the same kind of ugly sweatpants he'd waltz around in. Beauty, I wanted to tell him, just is. You haven't done anything to earn it. You can't wear it like a medal. And if you can wear it like a medal, then it's a medal you're going to lose. The loss was already well underway. Baby was far from the man he used to be, and when I saw his crow's feet I knew they were related to why he wanted to leave me. It was the money and his fading beauty, because Baby had caught wind of the loss. Baby only had one form of capital and that was the erotic. He wasn't talented, rich, or well educated. He wasn't particularly funny, sporty, or kind. Baby was erotic and women wanted to lie down next to him, and soon he'd be bankrupt.

Baby's name was on the rental contract, but we were both registered to the address and I was the one who'd found it. This life of contacts and shortcuts had never been his, and I suppose I could let him go but then he'd go back to where he came from – to ordinary life, an ordinary person's life. There was no way he'd be able to keep what was mine and be rid of me.

'Sure, Bibbs, you hooked us up with the apartment, but without me we wouldn't have been able to keep it.'

The tone between us had become hostile, and Baby was following me around as I searched for who knows what. He was wearing his impossible face. I felt combative.

'How long have you been planning this?'

'Bibbs, don't start. I can't get into yet another fight with you. You can stay here until you find something else and I'll help you look. Anyway the rent is too high for you on your own.'

'The rent isn't "too high for me", you idiot. I have savings.'

Baby, who had picked up the day's newspaper from the rug in the hallway, hurled it at the wall behind me.

'OK, fine, Bibbs, since your finances are so fucking solid, buy me out of the contract.'

'That's illegal,' I said, picking up the newspaper and carrying it to the kitchen.

'Here's a solution for you. You have money. Use it. For 100,000 I'll sign the contract over to you and move out.'

I chewed the inside of my cheek and searched for a different subject to fight about, but I was out of ideas. The day had come when there wasn't anything left to dredge up. Except this: who would leave who. Baby said, My God. My God just admit you don't have a single krona saved.

'You'll have the money in one week,' I said and walked past him on my way to the bathroom. His arm brushed against mine. I wanted to press up against him, but instead I locked the bathroom door and turned on the tap just as Baby had done each time he went to the bathroom during our four years together. As soon as I said 'one week' I wanted to take it back. One week was tight, but I'd set my own deadline and

Baby was already doubting me. Taking it back was unthinkable. If there was money, as I had claimed, there was no
reason to wait. One week was long enough, even if transferring from investment funds probably took a while. I couldn't
get out of this. The lie needed to dissolve into truth. I tried to
think and rinsed my face with so much water that two of the
fake eyelashes I'd applied fell off and stuck to my cheek. OK,
he could leave me and he could take Slipgatan but he'd never
get me to admit I didn't have a way out. I wasn't about to let
him play the hero, when he was the one ruining everything.

On the eve of Baby's fortieth birthday we were in raptures
and it was one of those countless nights on which he'd taken
up drinking again. We lit a dozen candles in the middle of the
table, and the wax ran across the white tablecloth in inscrut-
able patterns. On the other side of this locked bathroom door
he wasn't in raptures anymore. At least I'd succeeded in this,
I thought with schadenfreude. There he stood with his lumpy
nose, tan bordering on sunburn, crow's feet deepening, and
shoulders narrower than when we'd met, back when he was
still fighting for youthful vitality. But his mouth was still
full. Red. Hot. I carefully dried my face so as not to do more
damage to my eyelashes. I wanted him to hurt in the same
place I was hurting. I wanted to take my headache and give it
to his head. I wanted to tell him that I'd never said anything of
consequence to him, that even if I'd written 1,000 emails I'd
never expected a reply. I wanted to confess that the medal of
beauty had never been his. It was mine, and it was beauty that
excused his impotence, his self-pitying way, his low-paying

22

job, his drinking. I also wanted to say: 'I anticipate your thoughts before you even know you're about to have them.' But I decided not to say anything, because I hadn't anticipated him leaving me.

Lined up in Plexiglass boxes, above the sink, were my lipsticks. Their cases were black, gold, rosy metallic. Next to the cases stood glass bottles with pipettes and screw-top plastic tubes and every routine I'd embarked on but couldn't afford; they were taunting me. Routines, as if I were the beautiful one. Or perhaps the routines confirmed that I never had been. The wind whined in the haunted drain and I looked at my armpits, blotchy from my fading spray tan. I'd been convinced that I'd be the one to leave him.

He was standing so close to the bathroom door I almost hit him when I opened it. The surprise of Baby breaking up with me seemed to make the contours of his body sharper, sexier. My resistance softened. I didn't want to provoke him. I wanted him to take pity on me and take off his sweater and lie down on the sofa. When Baby got angry he clenched his jaw and fists. When he got caught in a lie his eyebrows shot into the air. The first time he put his cock in my pussy, he said: 'I'm freaking out.' When he beat himself in the face he would strike his sculpted cheekbone just below his left eye, but I didn't know what he looked like then because I'd always turn away.

'If you're wondering why I'm so surprised,' I said, the sobs draining from my throat to my stomach and bleeding into my arms and legs, 'it's because I'm much better than you, everybody thinks so.' He dropped his arms, which he'd reached out, ready for an embrace. I gathered up a few things that didn't belong together and shoved them into the Louis Vuitton bag I'd bought in Hong Kong.

'Bibbs, come on. Don't be such a fucking child.'

'Don't say my name. You'll have your money next weekend at the latest. I'll be in touch.'

The draught picked up right as I was about to slam the door, sabotaging the dramatic effect. Instead the door knocked up against the cushion of air and snapped at me like an angry mouth. The door made me think of our first happy summer together when I'd left all the windows and doors open, waiting for a draught that never came. That summer was windless and welcoming, just like this summer, but now without the welcoming part.

Yes, I'd left the apartment in a rush and was standing outside the entrance to Slipgatan holding my LV, crestfallen. I was used to being the one who caved and went back, but this time turning back wasn't to be desired. A younger girl walked by with a pizza box and did a double take when she saw me. The smell of pizza reminded me of being young one summer a long time ago, when friendships were more interwoven. I'd put on my comfy sandals and was walking to Västerbroplan, over the difficult bridge with the self-righteous cyclists. People came walking from Rålambshovparken, chill and not wearing much, some in high spirits but slow-going, swept up by the heat and tipsy from just a single glass of wine. As happens. Boys out and about in sweatpants and nothing on top, and girls whose under-eye concealer was a shade too light.

I got on the bus and rode it to Odenplan. A woman gave me a thumbs up and I thanked her and smiled. Grateful as hell. When I got off the bus I thought for a while about which way to go before I started shuffling down Odengatan so as to give someone sitting on a streetside patio a chance to recognise me. Tonight it had to be their treat, but everyone seemed to be caught up in their own thing. At the Italian restaurant there was no one I knew, and no one who knew me. Same at the Irish and at the Indian. On the curb, patrons were smoking, still not drunk enough to shout my name. I tried to figure out where to go. The lie about my savings had gone on for so long that it felt true, but however I twisted it, it wasn't. I'd had 100K before, more than once. But I hadn't saved it.

When no one at Wasahof tried to catch my eye, I turned back and thought about big jobs I'd done and wondered how those jobs had come so easily. Outside Tennstopet's restaurant patio I opened the calculator on my phone. I had eight on a credit card. I typed in 8,000. I had a think. OK, eight. I put the phone in the back pocket of my shorts. Eight on credit and no Baby. I had a gig on Tuesday. For that I'd invoice ten, but I didn't need a calculator to add those numbers up. I hadn't smoked for months, but as soon as I smelt that sweetness I knew it was time to start back up. Resistance took effort, and this crisis demanded my all. Sometimes you might as well start smoking again or eating or drinking, because obsessing over giving in or not giving in was a virus that infected the brain and clouded your thinking. Imposing bans and lifting them had kept me occupied for years. I asked a man who was smoking by the crossing for a cigarette, and he lit it for me without agitating for further conversation.

The white shirt I put on before I left Slipgatan smelt faintly of an Italian perfume oil. When I thought about how much the perfume cost, my stomach dropped, and that heaviness mingled with the smoke. I exhaled through my nose, the cigarette snug between my fingers. It hadn't been months since my last cigarette. I'd smoked last week. I thought about the perfume again. In business breaking even is key, and I wanted to rationalise away my anxiety about the perfume with my savings tactic. I'd polished that savings tactic to perfection. If a perfume had cost me 3,000, I'd work hard to get each krona back. Yesterday I bought a bra at 25 per cent off and saved 200 kronor. I could subtract those 200 from the perfume and so now it had cost 2,800 kronor. I went on listing my recent expenses. I'd taken the bus here, to Tennstopet. So I'd saved on cab fare, which would have cost at least 200. This meant the perfume was now down to 2,600 kronor.

I thought about how I'd invoiced for 800,000 the year of that happy summer, and I still took that sum as a landmark for how good we could be. That happy summer had played itself out in the illegal sublet in Hagaparken – a large yellow stone house with a lush garden – and when the rain stopped in July we stepped out into the garden and could hardly believe our eyes. Peaches were growing along the wall. At night field mice ran under the wooden boards, and Baby told me not to be afraid, so I wasn't and fell back asleep, dreamt that I was breathing through a ventilator in my throat. I woke up gasping for air. Before he moved in, I'd never been out in the garden, but he got me to do lots of things I hadn't done

27

before. I had just turned thirty-five and was wondering if I'd get pregnant. When we slept together I could feel my biology drawing him deeper in, and when he came inside me it felt like the orgasm was my own. His hot cum slid down my thighs when I went to the kitchen to make him a sandwich. The days were crazy hot and I felt like stabbing anyone who threatened him, and we took walks in the greenery around the building in the evenings, each with a stick in our hand, shouting rhymes at each other that he remembered from childhood.

'May I call you "brother"?' I'd whispered on the jetty at Brunnsviken, and the buzzing of gnats in the reeds was like a thing you were supposed to remember but hadn't bothered to write down. 'This will be our happy summer if you let me call you "brother".' Baby didn't get it and said, Don't say brother. Say darling, and I wanted to give him everything so I said: OK, darling. OK.

I didn't work hard for my money, and we never thought this happiness would end. Instead of counting on its end, we conjured grand fantasies of a shared future in Los Angeles and Berlin. Baby referred to himself as my wife, and I knew I could be whoever I wanted to be if I saw myself the way he saw me. He offered me an irresistible stability. I was still blogging our first year together, posting five times a week; one post would be about what I was buying and the next would be about how you didn't need to buy anything. During the spring, the show I'd shot the year before was broadcast – eight semi-famous participants eating dinner around a table. The show's concept was to create intimacy between the viewers and peripheral public figures; of these eight I was the brightest star and reached through the screen with my free-and-easy way. If you didn't know who I was before, you were finding out now. I was a size 40 and didn't pay for anything and I had managed to do my lips without it showing. It had just been an election year and I managed to encapsulate some sense of national dignity because on the programme I'd put a racist cast member in their place. I'd never been political before, but times had changed, civil courage was demanded of anyone who laid claim to space. One of the evening papers, *Aftonbladet*, ran a television column saying that apparently even a silly format such as this one could contain something of value. The column was about me.

During this time we'd walk into the city centre a couple of nights a week to see if the places we'd abandoned for each other still existed. Baby hated those middle-class haunts, but I'd walk through the door with one hand on back of his neck, and in the other a knife. No one was going to say a word about my Baby, and I told him not to be afraid, and he said he wasn't, but sometimes I could tell that he was. I'd love us more then. We drank in love, and strangers interrupted our embraces just to say that they worshipped me. Baby's eyes lit up as if they were talking about him.

Baby was on an hourly contract and barely worked that first year so that he could go everywhere with me and laze around with me in bed in the mornings. Shoes and winter coats arrived by courier with handwritten notes in a familiar tone from PR-agency employees. Baby took pictures of me in the garden wearing the shoes, and he'd take as many as I liked. The greenery was so green it was like a shining white light and I sat on the garden furniture, relaxed. He never tired of seeing me on screen. Here, I said and handed him the most expensive garments, give them to your sister. Overwhelmed, he kissed me, his tongue in so deep I couldn't breathe, as though he were trying to retrieve something. Afterwards he said he'd never done that with anyone else.

The money came so easily that summer that I, when left to my own devices, felt like a joke. As if I were selling something that was out of stock. But I was rarely left alone. Baby took care of the practicalities for me and I the magic for him. Unfortunately my accountant wasn't aware of this arrangement, and his emails telling me to stop spending the money that was supposed to go into my tax account were sent in vain.

Come autumn, when we could still trick ourselves into thinking that summer would return with one last gasp, I was given the opportunity to rent Slipgatan because the landlord's daughter had been following me from the start. I decided to leave the house in Hagaparken in order to become a woman with Baby. Because I had several demerits with the enforcement office, he was the one to sign the contract, but we told each other it belonged to both of us. The heart of our very first home was a king-size bed I gave Baby as a seven-month-anniversary present. The bed was almost two metres wide and cost 50K. At night we slept so tightly interlaced it might as well have been half a metre wide.

Right as I decided to head back to Slipgatan someone finally called my name. There on the patio sat Nina, an actress from Örkelljunga who had moved to Stockholm after she had her breakthrough. Her success was a mystery to me. The older I got, the more it seemed that who made it and who didn't was about something that predated adulthood, decided long before we had a chance to perform. Nina was dressed in ditzy florals because she indulged in a kind of pornographic countryside nostalgia, always directed at eyes that were keen to criticise her. During the spring she'd had the lead role in a web series on SVT, and she would write to tell me that I was brave, a kind of pioneer, and my blog (when it still existed) was a light in the darkness of low self-esteem. We were both fat. That's why Nina wanted us to be friends and me to be friendly. Being overweight suited her, as it suits all women under thirty. Me, I'm not so into being fat, I'm always trying to get skinny, but these are different times. Nowadays we're supposed to carry our shortcomings like strengths, as though we'd gone out and bought them ourselves. Nina got up and said a gushing, jumbled hello.

'Bibbs, fancy seeing you here!' Yes, Nina, fancy that, and I thought about the pizza that had walked past me outside of Slipgatan and how I used to simply pick up the phone and call my friends. Her breasts rested in the low neckline of her dress, unconcerned.

'Mind if I take a seat?'

Her friend was just leaving and Nina ordered me a vodka soda, and French fries, even though I'd said no thank you. I dutifully ate a fistful. We sat on the corner of Odengatan and Dalagatan with nothing to talk about. The crossing was playing its signal and Nina was saying something about the legacy of a feminist comic book artist who had taken her own life. Because Nina's worldview was absolutely correct and her opinions were streamlined, it was easy for me to get lost in thought, and I turned around in my chair when I heard new guests arriving, searching for better company than Nina. My glass was already empty, and Nina looked embarrassed when the waiters, who were well dressed but rude, walked right past her raised hand for the third time. The ice was the cheap kind that melted as you drank and clustered as chips at the bottom of the empty glass. I noticed that her face had changed. I couldn't say what she had changed. You never can. One day a face just looks less like the person it belongs to and more like a general sort of face, a collective face of indeterminate age, available to any woman who can afford it. Maybe it was the cheekbones, like two embedded fish fingers or the exaggerated point of her chin. Three strangers came up to her and none to me. She was twenty-nine. It didn't matter. She could have them. I'd already had them. I knew all about them. One of the strangers turned to me and said: 'You look familiar,' drawn out, as though we actually knew each other and not just him me.

Nina had a perverse fantasy about us being similar, or that a similarity would arise if we claimed it was there. Tacky city jeeps drove past as she desperately tried to find a subject that would engage me. Baby used to ask me to take pictures of him in front of vehicles that weren't his. Sunken into myself

32

I heard Nina once again bring up how similar we were. I told her: I'm supposed to say things like that to you, not the other way around. In the pictures I took, Baby was crouched down in front of large tyres and I came to think of the play of muscle across his thighs, moving in time with the clicking crossing signal. Or had it been more slowly? My memory was already failing and now he was on his way out, along with the pain.

'We're sisters,' she said, 'like all women are sisters.' I had another drink. Even though she was at the start of her success, and I at the end of mine, I was the important one of us two, which she gladly acknowledged. This explained her nervous way. Nina said she'd read my blog 'religiously' when I was still blogging, and that I was so good on TV. I didn't like hearing it. I didn't like hearing anything anyone had to say to me about me.

'You're, like, so confident. Unafraid.' I was already finished with my drink and the waiter with his glasses shoved down his nose took my order. The cars drove past more slowly the later it got, as if they were looking for someone who was sitting here. Nina said, 'I read it religiously,' again, swaying.

'Don't you want kids?'

I helped myself to a portion of snus from the tin on the table, sticking the little pouch under my lip and shrugging. Maybe at some point in the future. She asked me how old I was and I reluctantly replied that I was turning thirty-nine on Thursday.

'If I got pregnant today I'd keep it,' she said wistfully. 'I've always dreamt of being a young mother, even if it's already too late. Would you judge me if I had a baby now?'

33

Everything she said was so incomprehensible, but yes, of course I'd judge her. I bit my tongue and took another sip of my drink. She had contracted herpes, she said, leaning over the round café table, almost tipping it over. All of a sudden she had crossed the line between agreeably tipsy and annoying. I didn't mention my herpes and let her go on about hers. I didn't have to give them everything. My herpes was mostly in my ass and on my butt cheeks. She'd only had the one outbreak and today she found out what it was. But don't tell anyone, she said. No, of course I won't. Guess it's one of those things you'd never feel ashamed of, she said. Nah, I said. Probably not. Where were you headed? she asked, as though the answer were of no interest to her. I said:

'Oh, I was just out for a walk and then you caught sight of me.' What luck. What luck. Around her neck was a pearl necklace, and when she caught me looking she covered it with one hand.

'A graduation gift from my mother.' The hand was to protect the pearls, but I wasn't about to yank them off her. She was sloppy drunk. Sloppy Nina in the wet night who had left the day behind her without so much as a thought. Baby's gold signet ring on his ring finger. The jewellery people were given by the people who loved them.

'Bibbs, I really want to work with you. And not let all that shit come between us. I've always wanted to work with you. . . Maybe you could write something for me sometime. A series.'

I didn't know how, but how hard could it be to dream up a story and tell it? It was hard for me to show Nina, but it made me happy. Someone was thinking of me. She knocked her glass over, and I snatched my phone from the table and wiped it dry on my jean shorts. Jean shorts. I really liked the series she had done on SVT, which seemed to have nothing to do with this person here. Which must mean that she was a talented actress. Even if this night were the climax of her success, she would have left something behind, a series and a script with her name above the line. My climax came and went with me. The alcohol had weighed my body down instead of lightening it up, as can happen, my mind too.

'Of course I'll write something for you,' I said, and started dreaming a little.

'You've never really ever dug your heels in with anything, have you?' she said. Her phone lay wet on the table next to the bill.

The patio at Tennstopet was flushed with infrared heat and so were Nina's cheeks. I went to the toilet. My stomach felt queasy, but all I did was pee. The staircase's green steps reminded me of a kind of man I sometimes longed for, who I'd seen on TV. A Brit. I stumbled the last bit. Back at our table I inhaled the rest of the French fries. When the waiter came out for last orders Nina made me promise to go back to hers for another drink. She grabbed hold of my arm. Her nails were unvarnished. 'You can't go yet, Bibbs,' she said, not panting, but clear, a sober voice pushing through the drunkenness. As though I had no choice. 'We still have a lot to talk about.' I promised to go with her, and it was one of the simpler promises I'd made. But like everything else a person does, I'd come to regret it.

35

Nina was subletting an apartment on Västmannagatan
from a musician named Anton, a man who was wild about
women in an old-fashioned way. I'd always liked him because
Baby did not. She was paying 12,000, and I didn't set her
straight about the fact that she was getting screwed. The
hallway was long and cut through the whole apartment. She
took two low-ABV beers out of the fridge; a row of ants was
marching across the sink.

'I know,' she said when she saw that I saw, but she couldn't
know. We'd never see another nightfall. We sat down in the
living room and Nina kept on talking, in a forced way, about
everything that popped into her mind. She was attractive
of course, all actors are, and they talk passionately about
everything they don't know. They think their commitment
makes up for a lack of intelligence. That's why actors sometimes laugh so hard they roll on the floor, legs in the air. In
Nina's case, the extra weight was forgiving. But her symmet-
rical face was genetics and Juvéderm, not talent, I wanted to
hold that in mind. I really wanted to know it, in my soul. Her

red hair had been blow-dried with a round brush and she kept a little coke in a matchbox. I didn't have the energy to take coke, but I didn't have the energy to say no either, so I picked up a key. Nina was delighted.

'It's so fun partying with you,' she said. Her lower lip quivered.

'You're almost like a big sister,' she said with that lip. 'That's why I'm so glad to have the chance to talk to you now.'

The lamp on the ceiling was on and I was wearing my sandals. We'd never met up just us before and Nina was talking about how guys hate wearing condoms. Everything she said belonged to a life that was long since over. Don't make me go back there, I prayed. I thought about how Baby had looked in the window when I was leaving. Turn around, I'd prayed, but hadn't waited to see if he'd heard me. What if he'd actually turned around and I was gone? Everything was ruined. I wanted to call him, as if my fingers were what was aching and not my heart. My stomach was still upset and rumbling loudly. The bump of coke hadn't landed well. It would never be dark again, the sky was just a different blue. Nina smiled at me when she heard my stomach and put a record on. 'I hate music,' I said. She laughed. It wasn't supposed to be funny. The bathroom is next to the bedroom, she said in female solidarity.

In the bathroom I shit a river and because I'd eaten jalapeños that morning, there was a searing pain in my asshole that shot up my back. It felt like my anus had opened up and I was pissing shit out of the hole. The sweat was pushing through my forehead and streaming down my face. I considered crying. The music was playing loudly and in the bathroom time was set to a different clock, because it was impossible to determine how long I had been sitting there. But there I was, looking at my painted toes resting neatly in my sandals, while the last few days emptied out of me. When we'd sit on the couch, Baby used to put my feet on his lap and concentrate on painting each of my toes, even the little one that barely had a nail. When he was done, he'd kiss the top of my foot and blow on the polish. What was the point of crying. I wiped myself carefully and gently, but noticed I wasn't done. The shit kept flowing. I, Bibbs, had nothing to do with the shit, or at least was helpless to stop it. I dropped the paper into the bowl and waited to regain control of my body. Was this what it felt like to die. Completely at the mercy of the body's demise. A new song was playing in the living room and I picked up a wavy women's magazine next to the toilet. Nina's name was among the cover lines. 'I've chosen contentment,' she was saying in the pull quote. She sounded resigned. But that's where those cunts want us.

Even for a million kronor, I wouldn't have been able to say how long I'd been in there, because with the toilet beneath me, the day wasn't behind me, nor was the morning ahead of me. Nina shouted is everything OK? Terrified, I shouted back that it was. Under no circumstance was she to stand outside. The bathroom was a vacuum where nothing but this was happening. Had any sun been shining in, I would have seen the motes of dust frozen in the air. No shared jokes or conciliatory words, only shampoo bottles that had fallen off the rim and into the bathtub. When I finally managed to get up to flush, the handle came off in my hand. I looked at the handle and then at the toilet, the tank released a gentle stream of water. Nothing that gentle could flush this shit down, the huge pile of it. Everything was brown and green. Nina was singing along to the song playing in the living room. I pulled out a metre of paper from the holder and put it in the toilet, closed the lid. Of course I would have done things differently, if I'd taken the time to think this through. But time was of no concern to the bathroom or the person inside it. Luckily, I'd left my bag in the hall and my slide sandals were on my feet, and I slipped out into the stairwell. Night had come and gone, and the morning light greeted me, invigorating as only a new day can be. I pushed back against the building door, easing it shut to prevent a bang that could be heard inside Nina's, where she was waiting for me to come out of the bathroom and do another bump. The temperature was pleasant and I decided to jog all the way to Fridhemsplan. After running a few hundred metres, I waved down a taxi and jumped in.

I had Elahe's permission to sleep in her apartment at Kronobergsparken when she and her husband were on holiday. When I got there around four in the morning, I missed her very much. I emailed my agent Mickey while lying on her bed. 'Get back to me asap,' I wrote, deleting 'asap' several times before deciding to keep it. The request sounded like a command, but I was desperate, and the hardness I'd thought was inside me had softened. The panic kept creeping. No, Bibbs, I said to myself. Pull yourself together. You have to be your own dyke to the sea. If Baby had got ideas about me, I was going to show him that he had misjudged me, and when I was done he would think I was the one who'd left him, not the other way around.

Nina had written to me several times and then stopped, in the midst of a series of questions. My guess was that she'd discovered what had happened and when I looked at one of her Stories again I thought I looked pretty, in that red light. Nina was younger of course, but I looked thin, thinner, next to her and I hoped Baby would see it too, and understand. Her last Story was not ideal. You could hear that I was drunk and one of my eyelids had drooped. I wanted to send her a message asking her to take it down, but it was better to pretend to be asleep.

Because I hadn't slept, a hangover hadn't yet set in, and instead I'd slipped into a compromised sobriety. As I squeezed my eyes shut, a movement Baby used to make with his hands while saying 'Come here' played on my retina. I would stab anyone who arrived in the night. 'You never have to be that dramatic when you're fully devoted to the occult,' Marite said, and in Elahe's bedroom I was overcome by just how much I missed her, too. The room was painted a serene colour, 'Silk Mill', and I'd gone along to pick it out on Roslagsgatan. Afterwards we bought shrimp at Baronen and one of Sweden's biggest podcasters had said hello to me, even though we'd never met before. He was known for being in love with his wife. When Elahe asked if he and I were friends, I shrugged to avoid saying no. Baby didn't eat shrimp, or lobster, oysters, mussels or crayfish. Neither freshwater nor ocean. I went through my phone, and saw that Nina had messaged me on every app. Where'd you go? she had written. Come back, she wrote later. I turned off the screen, disgusted.

Nina was ingratiating and exuded a feminine satisfaction that made me perceive her motives as murky. Even last night, when she'd been playing host, I perceived her as both bumbling and shrewd. The shrewd part was that she wanted to get at something inside me that belonged to me by claiming it was hers. The bumbling annoyed me, but I preferred it to the confidence that arose when strangers turned into acquaintances. I'd learnt that when strangers get to know a person they look up to, the initial nerves are replaced by arrogance, or haughtiness. The haughtiness stemmed from a disdain for being granted access to me, which left them disappointed by life's lack of magic. So I was happy to avoid Nina and other younger women, because nothing good came from bridging that gap. Or I'd go between being gushing and cold, to reinforce my mystique in their minds. Because whatever Marite said about a challenging mystique, there was also a simple one. I thought of Nina's toilet. That wasn't mystique. Or was it.

Under the covers, I unbuttoned my shorts and the button had left a red mark above my belly button. Baby thought I was too old for short shorts, but I was still younger than him. Elahe's duvet cover was so silky I could barely feel it on my skin, and I read Nina's message again, watching the short video clips. Who was she going to tell? I counted five mutual friends and then another ten who were friends of friends, or acquaintances.

'It's so much fun having exchanges with older women,' she'd said as we left Tennstopet. 'Older women who still have normal lives.'

Elahe's apartment reeked of money, and we hadn't really been good friends since I helped her supervise the move-in. As the men unloaded the large vehicle, I asked how much the apartment had cost and Elahe replied that she wasn't comfortable discussing money. Her husband, who hates her, told me it had cost 8 million as he directed me behind a big oak cabinet in the elevator. They wanted me to make sure the movers didn't damage the wood. The last time I visited Elahe, a neighbour opened the door while I was waiting for the elevator, as if he had been standing there for weeks, eye to the peephole, waiting for me. 'I know you're a TV star.' Thank you, I said. 'But don't slam the gate.' I said I don't even live here. 'No, but each time,' the neighbour said, 'your slamming wakes up the dog.'

Elahe wouldn't tell me how much the apartment had cost and she hadn't shared what she was making with me in years. When we were younger, she would call excitedly after every promotion and tell me about her new responsibilities and her pay rise, but then came the promotion when she stopped. I concluded that she had been given new duties after an anecdote she recounted at a big dinner party. While we were having a cigarette outside, I tried to congratulate her. 'Oh, it's nothing,' she said, changing the subject before I could ask any questions, and after that we never talked about money again. The one time I did ask, Elahe said she couldn't quite remember.

People who can't remember what they earn always earn over 30,000. Everyone else remembers down to the krona. People who don't want to reveal how much their things cost either think that they deserve expensive things more than others do, or they think they're a type of person who takes greater pleasure in pleasure and no one else can understand. I'd been there myself. I knew the kind of answers that could be given to the question of why some had so little while you yourself had so damn much.

But this Sunday I was not grudging. Now that Elahe and her husband were away, the apartment felt like it belonged to me, and the beautiful decor conveyed authority. When I saw the colours and materials, I wondered why I hadn't thought of buying some beautiful glassware to place in the window along with thick books and bowls of walnuts and dried fruit. I consoled myself by thinking that there's no art to being generous when you can afford it. 100,000 kronor loomed. What's 100,000 kronor in relation to this apartment? Milk money. Last year my tax bill was 170,000. My former accountant retired and the new accountant, a person who likes to do the right thing, flagged up a series of errors to the tax authorities.

'Deductions are not an exact science,' I tried to reason with my caseworker, but the full sum still landed at 170K. Although 170 felt like an insuperable spiritual mountain, I took care of it because Baby had recently cleared my debt, and I didn't want to undo his good deed. So as not to disappoint him, I worked under the table for a couple of months then on the books when I'd get home from that job. Baby was mad about the debt, but didn't offer to help, and I'd expected he would. I'd thought about it every day until it arrived. At the start of our relationship, I hadn't explained that I was also spending the tax and VAT and when the time came to pay, I'd simply have to roll up my sleeves. Why haven't you paid your share? he asked. Because I liked paying for him so much. I liked saying: 'Don't worry about it,' and on some

44

nights mean it. I liked taking out my card before he even had a chance to reach for his wallet, without ever asking for anything, but still counting how many times he allowed himself to be on the receiving end.

Another unexpected expense, the year before the year of the 170K, came after the retired accountant and I had deducted part of a friend's home as an office. One day, the tax authorities got in touch and told me that this did not add up. I called my caseworker and said my first and last name slowly into the phone. 'Everyone needs to do their part,' the woman said, and I wondered, if Baby had heard her say that, would he have wanted to sleep with her? Baby loved to say that everyone should do their part, and living with Baby meant wondering which women he wanted to sleep with.

In the 170,000-kronor year I had seven months, so now I was undeniably under more pressure, but acting in desperation had its pros and cons. I was used to racking up debt and lucking out.

The phone trembled with a new message. It was Nina, yet again wondering where I was and asking if I wanted to go for breakfast. I put the phone down, puzzled.

In a way, the distance to Slipgatan was like a migraine finally releasing. Like, it still hurt but not as much. The work of being the person who lived with Baby had taken all my time and all my money. Braided garlic, emerald-green velvet sofas, and evasive answers to direct questions. Shit like that. But it was my shit. At six o'clock, I was going to head for the Italian on Norrtullsgatan and order an Americano with a splash of hot milk for 39 kronor. An Americano shouldn't cost 39 kronor, but as soon as I had the thought, I knew it wasn't my thought. It belonged to Baby. He was careful with his own money, careless with mine, and always asked what everything cost, even if he already knew the answer. Sometimes he would tell me how many hours he'd have to work to pay for something I was buying, but this mindset couldn't be applied to me because neither of us knew how to make the calculation.

Right as I was beginning to suspect that my days of smooth sailing and free lunches would not last forever, I lost my accountant, and real talk, it was not because he retired. My accountant had gone to jail for running multiple shell companies. When Baby asked me why, I told him the same thing the accountant had told me: 'He needed the dough,' and in that way I felt a kinship with the accountant. One morning before the accountant went away, I'd stopped by his office and said that I was sorry, but I couldn't continue to be his client. 'You don't have to stop by the office to tell me that,' he'd said. 'I'll be billing you for this hour.'

He's pressed, of course, I'd told Baby that night when he was cooking and I was unwinding on the kitchen sofa. Baby hadn't turned around.

'Do you know that other people pay me for what I have to say,' I'd said, 'and you never even listen?'

Nope, he replied still with his back to me, they pay you to speak through you.

The accountant's measured tone during that office visit reminded me of a conflict I'd had with the bank around the same time, which the accountant left me hanging with when he closed up shop. I had to call to ask about my accounts myself, and I made a point of staying calm during the entire conversation, but it was that psycho-calm that women have learnt to employ around men, and finally I said, without a hint of the resignation I'd been feeling for weeks:

'I no longer want to be your customer,'

and the bastard on the other end of the line responded in monotone:

'I'll have you know that you being our customer only costs us money.'

I had no real sway. Low income was like minus sway, negative sway, and I couldn't buy shit with the shit that I got. Since then, the negative sway had only increased.

During the night, Baby had texted to say that I could change my mind about buying him out of the contract. He would even give me 25K if I moved out. The paint in Elahe's bedroom had cost 25, and I replied that I didn't want 25. I wanted my apartment. He replied in a tone I could tell was cunty: 'OK. Transfer the money soonest.'

A dream flew past, of an envelope with cash propped against the candlestick on the kitchen table, waiting for Baby to come home from work. On the envelope I had written in ink:

'It's over.'

Though had I actually been the one to leave him, my parting words could be more magnanimous.

'Thanks for a nice time. It's over.'

I punched the bed. I had found Slipgatan and made it into Slipgatan. I had my shop on Reimersholme where I bought lottery tickets. You don't jinx that sort of thing. The apartment was mine.

'Something will turn up via the housing list soon, right?' Elahe had said during a quick phone call. Elahe's vacation had been rattling in the background, and it was hard to glean the nuance in her voice. Did she feel sorry for me? Or did she think I was brave? I'd told her that it was me who left Baby, not the other way around. The truth, that he had left me, wasn't credible. To my surprise, she'd sounded relieved. Then the housing list was mentioned, but I couldn't be straight with Elahe. I wasn't on any housing list, because I'd always thought I would buy something. Why not? Stuff like that happened to people all the time.

'Or,' Elahe continued, alas in a solution-oriented mood, a mood for people with resources, 'you have so many contacts. I'm sure you can find a sublet in a jiff.'

There were several reasons why I wouldn't be able to rent something in a jiff, but what pushed its way to the top of the shortlist of good reasons (non-payment of debts, didn't want to) was the thread 'Face Filler Whore Elisabeth _____ busted for possession!' on Flashback.

WHEN THAT FACE FILLER WHORE ELISABETH GOT BUSTED FOR POSSESSION

Your girl bought two grams at Häktet, it was Elahe's birthday. It was only right. When the delivery arrived (took a while) Elahe and the others were tired, wanted to go home. I wrote to our hookup and asked if I could return the drugs. No reply. The feeling of embarrassment for having gone out of my way for someone who didn't care hounded me into the next week and I put off responding to Elahe's messages. Three months later, at dawn, the doorbell rang. A drug ring had been broken up. The police were reading text messages, I had sent several. 'Please, I haven't used any,' I'd written. 'I really need the money back, and you can sell the coke to someone else.' Is this you? I, for whom dragging out awkward replies is usually something of a talent, responded right away: Yes, that's me. Baby was listening from the bedroom. When I got back into bed, I pretended he was asleep and started pretend-sleeping myself. After a while, I fell asleep for real. An old track-and-field athlete who had started a PR agency and did the Sweden Democrats' election campaign emailed to say he knew how to bury information and to get in touch if I needed help. It hadn't seemed important. No one called me Elisabeth anyway and I didn't really think it was anything to be ashamed of. After the trial, I paid a few thousand in fines and felt anxious about the headlines for a few days, but went to the country with Baby, where we mostly talked about other things. A couple of weeks later the storm had calmed and, crisis or no crisis, I was still Bibbs. A name that stared back at me, questioning whether or not I belonged to it.

No, I had no desire to sublet something in a jiff. I was fucking middle-aged. The sun squeezed in through the gap at the
bottom of the blinds in Elahe's bedroom and I decided to
get up. In the apartment's other hallway, before the kitchen,
hung a full-length mirror that Elahe put away when she had
guests. How abstract, paying 8 mill for something, I thought,
and put the Nespresso capsule in the machine. How much
money did I burn through this month? It was mysterious.
How much was I pulling in? Even more mysterious, and the
biggest mystery of all was how I did it. I opened my mouth
to relax my jaw.

'I could die tomorrow,' I'd say to people when they said
something encouraging. I could die tomorrow, I'd said twice
during the phone call, louder and louder, because Elahe didn't
hear me the first time. When I repeated myself, the humour
of it lost its edge. Are you really managing on your own now?
she asked. I was trying to read her. Maybe she admired me.
    'Yes, yes. I have lots to do.' And boy, did I.

I preferred proper espresso, but no one had had a machine
like that at home in years. You have to spend your money
right, I learnt the hard way, after the verdict. Money is a
firebomb that shouldn't detonate in the wrong place. You
have to toss it in the right direction because money leaves
a trail that leads back to the person who wanted something
for their outlay. No, the fines and the headlines didn't bother
me; they were part of the story of Bibbs. On the other hand,

I kept thinking about a column on ideals and hypocrisy that had run in *Aftonbladet*. The writer didn't print my name, but those who knew, knew. Why don't our idols say anything meaningful, the lede read. After the reality show set around the dinner table, I'd spoken out in several interviews about how all people are to be valued equally and the importance of giving people a chance, things that didn't stem from me. Every time I took a position on something, I had a niggling worry that it was the wrong position, but my commitment meant that I was offered a pre-paid phone card ad. The images looked analogue and I was casually dressed in a grey-marled Champion sweatshirt, on a spring evening with Blåkulla's blue apartment blocks behind me. The sky was pink with stretched-out clouds like wisps of sand. On the way home after the shoot, I walked through the cemetery. The stones were hewn with children's names.

The point of the column was that I was profiting from the 'ghetto aesthetic' when I made the pre-paid phone card advertisement in front of high-rises but by buying drugs I had contributed to the gang violence that was destroying that place. Baby had tipped me off about the column but I didn't feel like they'd got me. The ghetto has no aesthetic? That's what those neighbourhoods are known for, silent rock upon silent rock above the washed-out hoodies heading for Willy's discount grocery store. But there was no point arguing against it, because people like that writer think everything has a hidden meaning, and that I, Bibbs, am contributing to said meaning. As if my 1,800 kronor for two grams would

have killed anyone, as if the dealer wouldn't have gone elsewhere if I hadn't got in touch. It felt a bit rich to claim that
I, Bibbs, had a responsibility towards a stranger who had no
responsibility towards me. Sure it didn't look good, because
if I have one currency it's credibility, but I never thought
anyone would get mad at the campaign both because there is
no such aesthetic and because everyone buys drugs at some
point sometimes, even those who rarely take them. Not to
mention, the fee was small. You buy drugs for your small
fee when the urge, a parasite, takes hold of your brain and
wipes out everything you've learnt and you let chaos reign
and you say that you'll navigate better in the chaos. What
remains is the night and the rules of the night. Like on Elahe's
birthday, I wanted to drag her down into the tar we used
to wade through together and that I was still stuck in. Like
some people call in sick because they have a hair appointment
or cancel a dinner by blaming it on their kids. That's exactly
how people buy drugs sometimes, in a melodramatic attempt
to rekindle a stagnant relationship. 'I shave my legs, is that
illegal too?' I asked Elahe when she'd finished reading the
column here in this kitchen, without comment. We sat there,
scraping our long nails against the tabletop. Elahe had grown
up in Blåkulla and I wanted to cover her lofty silence. I didn't
have it in me to explore what it contained, so I babbled on
about other things while she flipped through the paper, not
chiming in about how stupid the people were who were
against me. As if her proximity to those swimming-pool-
coloured buildings made her more important, or superior.
Freed from how much I had been missing her, I finished off

the Nespresso. I regretted having spoken out about the old man on TV being an Islamophobe. If I'd kept my mouth shut, they'd have cut out what he said, and no one would have expected me to do better than anyone else.

The phone buzzed on the kitchen counter.

'What do you call that tone?' Mickey said without saying hello. '"Asap" – we don't talk to each other like that, do we? How the hell are you? I'm in El Los Angelos! City of Angels!'

Well, Mickey, it's crisis time, you feel me. His voice came and went through the silence of the phone, as if the absence of sound between sentences was darkness and his voice a waning light.

'I've left Baby and he's taking the apartment if I can't come up with 100 grand.'

Mickey's voice resurfaced,

'You left Baby? What the fuck for?'

I sat down. 'I can't do this over the phone. Do you have anything in the works for me?'

Being straight with him, that I'd been left, was not possible. Mickey, as my agent, already thought I'd lost out on a lot and his belief that I was aspirational for women was, if not extinct, then at least under threat. My Baby was Mickey's last hope, because Mickey thought that a woman's status as an idol was measured by her age and the man at her side.

Mickey was a good friend, who wore tweed to parties and chewed nicotine gum. He had grown up in Stockholm like me

and used to run a music mag in the Nineties called *A.I.D.S.*
Mickey had hooked me up with a lot of gigs and was one
of the first people to see a potential income stream when he
looked at me. I started blogging at the age of twenty-five
and was quickly snapped up by *Expressen Fredag*. Back then it
wasn't yet possible to understand what the internet was and
that people were reading it, so I wrote exactly what I thought
about everyone I met and because I loved going to bars, many
of the people I met were, in a broad sense, famous. As compe-
tition was low, I became Sweden's biggest blogger for a time
and the bigger the blog got, the more reactions my thoughts
roused, thoughts that should have stayed in my head. Mickey
intercepted me at the Opera House and persuaded me to
leave the newspaper's platform and switch to a private one, so
he could sell ads. He got 20 per cent of everything. Mickey
always understood that just because we didn't go deep, we
weren't superficial. We wanted the same thing and snuck out
of parties together without saying our goodbyes. In addition
to being my agent, he handled a few other high-profile cli-
ents and musicians, but most of his income came from selling
stock lots he bought from a guy he went to school with.

Thanks to the blog, which I couldn't support myself with,
I got a job as a presenter on MTV, on a dating show with low
ratings called *XOXO*. Then the blog died. Not mine, but as
a phenomenon. So Mickey arranged for me to start blogging
on a women's magazine platform, so as to mature with my
audience. Then the women's magazine died. So I took up
Instagram, but Mickey had got old and instead of focusing

on building my brand, he encouraged me to do linear TV. So I made a family-friendly show which led to Baby falling in love with me, then I did another show, the year after the success of the first one. By then Baby and I had settled into Slipgatan and it was summer again. The night before filming started he punched through the plaster of the living room wall, beside himself with a longing that he was working through before he'd actually experienced it.

The show was filmed on a farm in Värmland and Baby called me every night and we'd argue on the phone until someone from the crew came walking through the dark, to where I was standing next to a gravel pit. On the other side of the farm was a lake with rippling rings that seemed to appear out of nowhere, but were in fact from the dragonflies reeling across the water's surface. But I wasn't surrounded by all that beauty as I was talking to Baby – they'd find me walking in the gravel and dust, which turned my shins grey. They'd remind me, voices tentative, that tomorrow would be a new day. It's hard to fabricate a hit and the programme came and went without anyone writing my name. I had stopped blogging because I ran out of material. Somehow, inexplicably, everyone I met up with was my employer. In addition, the blog felt like a pursuit for people younger or older than I was, but I didn't tell Mickey that – unwilling to draw attention to a change I couldn't control.

'I'm actually a writer first and foremost,' I would say to Mickey.

'Sure you are, Bibbs,' Mickey replied. Baby once said: 'I thought writers had to write in order to be writers.' But I meant that I was an all-around creative. For example: I exhibited work at a bar in Östermalm a few years ago. Watercolours, portraits of my friends. I spun records and played the sidekick for the presenters of various programmes, both radio and television, and made various public appearances. But nothing was as good as it had been on MTV, when I was on MTV. The world opened up if you were on MTV. For a while, it was impossible to imagine the world without MTV, and once I started, that chapter had unfortunately come to its end.

'We didn't know that we had it all,' a presenter from the network said to me while drunk, when I was brand new.

'We who?'

You and me, he replied, but I suspected he meant other people. After we downed shots served in test tubes and sang karaoke, he fingered me. I could hardly believe that he wanted me, because when you're young you don't know that youth is the most attractive thing a person can be in possession of and that everyone who's on the cusp of ageing covets it. The presenter was short and fit, and, with his face pressed to my neck, I could see that he had dyed his hair dark. The colour had stained his pale scalp.

'You're so wet,' he gasped into my hair, and a thought flashed through my mind that he was fake.

I've never been as hungry as I was then. We spent our days in the MTV studios down in Frihamnen, working more or less for free. As for me, I didn't have a television and had already aged out of the job, as my mother told me. I'm sure she was right. 'Where can I watch it?' she asked, and I asked my colleagues but got no real reply. In the staffroom was a sofa I recognised from one of the more popular shows, a show that had unfortunately been cancelled after they gave a dog the job of presenter. Between the sofa cushions were the sound guys' coins and I gathered them up every Friday afternoon after everyone else had gone home, flat broke. One morning I stuffed a coin into my pussy and walked around with it inside me for a whole day. When I ran into the presenter who'd fingered me, I took the coin out and gave it to him. His jaw dropped. 'Put it in your mouth,' I said, and he did.

Mickey had never been that compliant and, speaking to him on the phone now, he sounded less worried than I'd hoped he'd be.

'Honey, we'll work it out, but lose the tone. It's a drag.'

I'd stood up and was shifting my weight from leg to leg, unsure if it was clear to him that I wanted him to handle it.

'What are you even doing in LA?'

'I'm on—' Darkness closed in around Mickey's voice, then the words pushed through. 'I'm on leave.'

Mickey had never taken time off and he hadn't informed me that he'd be going away, and we used to talk at least twice a week. I unclenched my jaw again. What if he was there working. Well, who with? I could name at least five girls off-hand who had moved there because their networks allowed it, but Mickey knowing them, or them knowing Mickey, was unlikely. Girls with Swedish followers who invested in their bodies in a big and American way. And so what if he was there working? Just because the idea of exporting my career had been a non-starter, its content self-referential and therefore requiring a Swedish canon for context, there was no reason his professional life should suffer.

'Time off,' I said, hoping Mickey hadn't heard what I'd heard, that I sounded defensive. Maybe he really was there for some R&R, even though he used to say it was nice not having a job because you never had to come back from vacation.

'How do we take care of this, Mickey? I'm down to my last krona.' He guffawed.

'Didn't you hear me: I'm away in the City of Angels? But sure, I'll sort something out. I'll have Texas call you as soon as he wakes up.'

Baby

If I were to draw my Baby's portrait, I'd do it in great detail, because the things I loved about Baby were not the things one might notice at first glance.

Well, there was his beauty, of course, but it had faded, or rather was wiped out, because he'd lost it over the course of two or three days. But he carried his beauty like a memory, which made him vulnerable and the vulnerability put one in mind of his beauty. At first glance, you thought he was still beautiful, but the longer you looked at him, the clearer it became that he was past his peak. The unruly hair on his head was now patchy and thin, and he'd taken to shaving it off. The back of his head was flat. He had bad posture, shoulders bent towards the ground as if by magnets. When he kept up his running, he had long, lean muscles, but he didn't run often because when he left me on my own for longer than absolutely necessary it made me unhappy.

If he picked the movie, it would be something by Tarantino or Woody Allen.

Above all, Baby was someone to love because I managed to be with him and he with me. Women in bars told me that they'd never seen him be so accommodating, their voices tinged with admiration and horror.

Baby was not normality itself but a symbol of it, and he served as an interpreter for the explanatory model that other people had of reality. He worked five days a week and on weekends he relaxed. He ran his errands. He used public transportation. He cooked and then he put his leftovers in a container, which he'd take to work the next day. He didn't call in sick unnecessarily. He drank to forget. He called some people and had others call him.

Baby liked going to the movies and sometimes I went with him. One night we were walking home after a movie on Sveavägen and ran into an actress, no older than twenty-three. The way she insisted on stopping to chat, along with his clumsy decorum, made it clear that they had slept together. That night I created an inner world of images, the first of which was a close-up of his face the very moment he came inside that young girl. His cock split her in two.

If I were to draw Baby's portrait, I'd be thorough, but vague. Baby's vagueness was one of his great strengths, and he'd agree with anyone he was talking to. The only thing he really stood by was not eating meat and this had become a fundamental part of his identity. On weekends he'd make me smoothies. He drank impressive amounts of alcohol but punished himself by getting up early in the morning after a rough night, and always said no when asked if he was hungover. When we first met, he liked doing things alone and it lent him an air of autonomy, which I did my best to break down. Once he cried soundlessly in Kungsträdgården when I tried to leave him. Our way of being with each other reminded me too much of a life I'd already lived and I thought I'd hit my limit. 'But you know me so well,' he said with his hands clasped, looking right into the sun and the high, clear sky so I wouldn't see. But I did see, and the rare tears that exposed Baby's brittleness made such an impression on me that I resolved never to leave him again.

I wasn't happy that Mickey had passed the buck to Texas and went into the master bathroom to scope out the medicine cabinet. Behind a glass jar of brushes, I found a bottle of Ritalin, the label ragged from condensation. Texas, who always wore short-sleeved shirts, was Mickey's husband. His long hair reached all the way down his back, and I didn't like him, he was the nostalgic type. But one thing I did envy him was his Crohn's disease. I'd watch him stuff himself with long Subway sandwiches, and wonder how it was possible for that bread not to leave a trace. Many of the girls who came up to me in town were pleased about my weight. 'It's so nice that you're not a size zero,' one girl said, and I, dumbfounded, wondered how she could possibly know. Sometimes Texas would bare his teeth and those receding gums and say: 'What are you looking at?' Nah, I don't know, but I wondered how someone who neither needed nor appreciated thinness got it so easily. I shook three pills out of the bottle, did a rough calculation in my head, shook out another three, swallowed two and wrapped the others in a piece of paper. I put the jar back on the wrong shelf intentionally. I wouldn't want Elahe to think that I'd taken the pills on the sly.

Even though I didn't like Texas, we often spent time together while waiting for Mickey. Texas and Mickey had been a couple for fifteen years. They lived in the same apartment but no longer shared a bed (Mickey was a sleepwalker) and celebrated birthdays but not Christmas. Texas had a way of walking into a room that had made Mickey fall in love many years ago. I'd never seen Texas walk into a room, he was always already there when I arrived.

The basement room out of which Mickey operated was thoughtfully equipped with office supplies and served both as the locale for Mickey's agency and as a boutique. Mickey and Texas each had a desk, and Texas was Mickey's assistant, driver, and cook. Everything on Mickey's desk was bigger than the stuff on Texas's. The desk itself was bigger. The letter tray was bigger. The picture frames were bigger and his ergonomic chair even had a headrest. Everything Mickey sold was neatly displayed in cardboard boxes and on bookshelves, and pinned to the walls were press clippings. The clips were mainly interviews I'd done in *Veckorevyn*, *Style By* and even *DN*. A few of the clips were about other girls, but not as many. The apartment above Mickey's basement room was noisy and sometimes the noise led Mickey to talk about his children, who none of us had met.

I never used to feel a kinship with Mickey and Texas, but a sense of solidarity had grown over the years. I began to glean what had happened to them and how. As I stood with the toilet-paper-wrapped Ritalin looking back on my life, this morning seemed inevitable. I was alone, again. I had a few thousand on credit and furniture I'd bought with pre-tax funds. I'd done my face, but it wasn't permanent. I'd done my nails, but they weren't permanent. Neither were the hair, the wax job, the dry-cleaned clothes, or the projects. Nothing in my life except the credit card bills pointed to a future that could be foreseen.

Elahe's living room was a beautiful room with parquet floors. The room was so large that the dining table had been placed in its middle, a table with an untreated wooden top and pink marble legs. The chairs were hard Italian plastic, to contrast the natural materials. Nothing was mine. Nothing except the realisation that nothing turns out the way you imagined it would, no matter how carefully you imagine it. I looked at Elahe's map of the world hanging above the sofa, thinking. . . You think that once you unfold 'it', a perfect picture will be revealed. Instead, you see a misshapen map with arrows pointing every which way, and wherever you go, there you are.

I hadn't taken much with me from Slipgatan. In the bag were a pair of tights and some panties, clean and dirty. My computer. I made Elahe's bed and checked my phone. No emails. The road outside had come to life. Cars jostled with buses and the siren from an early police call rose towards the sun, whose bright morning light obscured the computer screen. I didn't have it in me to wait for Mickey to call, so I messaged Texas, who was already awake. He would be in the office after lunch. It was almost seven o'clock. If there's one thing I'll get done today, I told myself while rummaging through Elahe's make-up box, it's buying a blender. Baby wasn't the only one who could make smoothies. I thought about the money, and yes, about being alone again. I'd get my hands on 100,000 if it was the last thing I did. If sadness swooped in, I'd slap it away. My mind on other things, I let my hand caress my other hand. Imagine if the body could be such a thing, sexual. Not just a work thing or a porn thing or a drunk thing. A thing you caress your way into. Sometimes, when I found a video made by a real couple, I might catch a glimpse of hand caressing hand, tenderly. Or a hand caressing a pussy the way the hands of any man in love caress a pussy. As if they were submitting to it, and a man can only submit to a woman willingly. I knew all this. How I could then carry out my plan so rashly can only be explained by the knife lodged in my heart.

'Bibbs! what are you doing here?'

I was there because it was Cash-Grab Day, but I couldn't say that, not yet; instead I suggested breakfast in town. Kenneth stood in front of me, newly awake, wearing only American boxers. My make-up was flawless, and I had done everything else flawlessly too. Kenneth was just over fifty, lived in the same building as Elahe, was tall and lanky, with conical pecs. When I suggested he start working out, he said that exercise increased oestrogen in men, which made their pecs bigger, but his tanned arms had an inviting boyishness and he spoke in a rural dialect as a joke, to seduce women. He'd recently lent a large sum of money to a mutual acquaintance who was in a legal dispute over botched construction. Ooh, I'd thought when I heard that, so the old man has money-money.

We'd known each other for a decade, but as the irritation I'd cultivated for Kenneth blossomed into contempt, Baby ended up being the one he'd hang out with, which had been going on for some time. But it was Cash-Grab Day, so my personal feelings didn't matter. Since I wasn't going to be able to buy my EuroJackpot ticket in the shop near Slipgatan, I had to make the most of this day. Kenneth went back into the apartment and re-emerged fully dressed and we didn't speak until we were out on the street. He lit a cigarette and I felt overly optimistic, as if I already had the money in my account. Baby would be surprised when I called to tell him that it was sorted, maybe even a bit humiliated or at least unsure if he actually knew me as well as he thought he did.

Kenneth walked a few steps ahead of me, the way all men always walk a few steps ahead of their female companions. We walked down Sveavägen. I was charming and upbeat, mimicking the few people we passed on the street and telling hilarious anecdotes, always at my own expense. Kenneth turned and looked at my breasts, excited that I'd showed up without Baby, but didn't ask why. When I rehashed my encounter with the man who'd brought bouncer's choice to Stockholm, he shook with laughter and suggested amorously that we should have a baby.

'You already have children,' I replied, not sounding ungrateful.

'But none that I want. Ours would have turned out great.' He plucked a small piece of tobacco from his tongue.

The cafe on Norrtullsgatan had just opened and the owner said 'Buongiorno.' The walk there was ugly. Wretched. Elahe's ADHD medicine had snuck up on me and I was having a hard time focusing on Kenneth. Every single sound in the room took up equal space and I held my breath in an attempt to ground myself. I rattled on about whatever was flying through my mind, about my nails and carbohydrates, about pornography. A new mother had taken a seat at the table opposite and I broke down breastfeeding porn into three categories: tender, BDSM, incestuous. That's how you get help, I'd learnt, by appearing as if you don't need it. But the light-hearted mood of the walk was slipping out of my hands and my rundown did not amuse Kenneth, although I knew he often watched pornography and even bought it on DVD.

Kenneth had finished his Americano and I hadn't touched mine; however, I had moved my chair so close to him that I was practically sitting in his lap. I leant back and excused myself to the ladies. When I returned, Kenneth had ordered another coffee and two croissants, and I remembered that I was hungry and immediately bit off half. Pastry flakes dusted my vest and Kenneth looked at my breasts again. I tried to bring the conversation around to money.

'So, I hear you've got into construction? Mick told me you helped him with the bathroom.'

Kenneth dismissed it with a wave,

'Oh, it was just a loan for a few weeks. Nothing worth mentioning.'

'You're almost too generous! You know that's not the only reason we like you, Kenneth.'

Kenneth didn't pick up on my flattery; instead he picked up his phone. I waited for him to say something, to ask how I was or ask about my own bathroom, to say something that might serve as an opening for him to offer me money without my asking for it. While he was scrolling, I tried to wait in silence without it seeming passive-aggressive. He looked up from his phone.

'How crazy is it that Mickey is in LA?'

I agreed, yeah so crazy. But, I back-pedalled, not that crazy really. After all, Mickey and I have a nice sum of money coming in. Kenneth drew his thin lips inward.

'You do?'

'Yeah, we always have money coming in.'

'The last time I saw Baby he said you hadn't worked all year.'

I didn't know what to say. I had been working, just not a lot. I had been on a bar tour and I had done three sponsored posts for a razor with a cardboard handle, the marketing of which was two-pronged: one, it was up to each woman to choose whether or not she wanted to shave; two I couldn't remember.

'Has he left you?'

'Who?'

Kenneth sighed,

'Has Baby left you, Bibbs? The man you live with?'

I chewed slowly until I realised I didn't have anything in my mouth.

'No, I've left him.'

Kenneth was more hunched over than usual, as if it would make him appear reassuring.

'Baby called me yesterday and said he left you, and that he's been trying to get hold of you, but doesn't know where you are or how you are.'

The croissant was gone. I reached for Kenneth's.

Kenneth had started a clothing brand in the late Nineties that had introduced Japanese denim to Stockholm. The lines had been straight and chaste, trousers so stiff they were like corsets. At the time, Stockholm thought it was a reaction to the hyper-sexualised Nineties, but having since got to know Kenneth, I knew that he just wanted to live out his perversion, his pathological obsession with women who have straight, slim bodies. At the time, jeans *were* something, however that happened. You had to put your trousers in the freezer and count the seams, and Kenneth was king of this psychosis and worked barefoot in his first shop.

Ten years ago, Kenneth sold the company but stayed on as creative director until his life was destroyed by a girl his colleague had taken on as an intern. He was made to leave by being told to request indefinite leave and since then he'd vacationed in Portofino twice a year and had repainted his apartment dark green. The other year, Åhléns purchased the clothing brand that had begun as a dream in his childhood bedroom in Vadstena, where Åhléns was the only shop. Åhléns was a department store that stood for everything he wanted to get away from (his mother and all the other middle-aged women), and when the sale went through he drank from morning till night six days in a row, until his daughter came to visit one afternoon and found him naked in the kitchen with a girl her age. She was in high school. Now the brand, Åhléns, was making stretchy jeans in washed-out colours.

Kenneth didn't seem to mind me eating his croissant; instead he took to folding the napkin that had been under the small plate with neurotic precision. The demon on Kenneth's back was that he was a bad man but would have preferred to be a good one. No, wrong. He didn't want to be a good man, he wanted to be perceived as good. My patience was wearing thin.

'For fuck's sake, Kenneth, no, he hasn't left me. Who do you trust more? Him or me?'

Kenneth didn't respond. I changed tack.

'I can't go into what happened, I don't want to hang him out to dry. But yes, it's true that he can't get hold of me. I know you've become pals, friends even. But Baby might not be who you think he is.'

'You two have been very much in love.'

The blade of the knife was being drawn from my heart down into my stomach.

'Yes. Or. Have we?'

The chair was getting uncomfortable. I wanted to change position but thought it might make me seem dishonest, so instead of freeing my legs, which were wrapped tightly around each other, I started talking about Slipgatan.

'That apartment is my only shot at having a place to live – I'll never rent anything above board, or take out a loan. I can forget about that.'

Another barista came out of the dish pit and took her place behind the counter. These fucking baristas have ideas about themselves. They think they're sommeliers, but really they're cashiers. Kenneth didn't disagree but didn't argue either. The wooden floorboards were long and unbroken, like a brilliant thought. It's been years since I had one of those, no lie, I told Kenneth, but he was clearly unhappy with my mood and pretended not to hear. I was furious that Baby had got there before me. That little whore had the nerve to leave me, when I was the one who was supposed to leave him, and now he was calling my fucking friends, pretending to be concerned. I had an idea of what he was up to. Baby wanted to stop Kenneth from giving me money. I had to make a plan, and before I had time to change my mind, I said the one thing Kenneth would have the hardest time openly disbelieving.

'He raped me.'

Kenneth opened his mouth, then shut it again.

'Yes, or. . . I don't know if you can be raped when you're in a relationship,' I pretended to think with my mouth half open, 'but he had sex with me against my will. The other week.'

'Five years in?'

The other night outside the café I'd seen two rats strolling along side by side, and was about to tell Kenneth but forced myself to return to the conversation.

'Four years, and it's happened before, right as we were getting together. But then he said that I'd misunderstood the whole thing and it would never happen again, and now it happened again. So I had to leave him.'

Kenneth's pained face convinced me that I'd struck gold, and inwardly, before I started to accuse myself, I built a strong defence. Could I do worse than accusing Baby of rape? Nothing was more embarrassing than raping someone, and Baby's dignity was virtually inviolable. With his honest job and the phone calls he took. And Baby had surely raped someone, at some point, and the other crimes he'd committed would sound minor if I recounted them. What was I supposed to say, that he'd left me but had no right to? Or should I say that I was brilliant and the brilliance had dulled because Baby had dulled it. That everything had been bright until it wasn't anymore. How could I prove that? Even if I could prove it, it wouldn't be worth 100K.

'Kenneth,' I put my hand on his, 'I need your help. I need a base. A home, and that costs money. It feels grotesque having to lay myself bare like this, to sit in front of you with my bloody wound, but if you want to know exactly how it happened,' I could feel Kenneth vibrating with anxiety and pleasure; I playfully tugged his index finger, 'I was asleep. I was asleep and woke up with him inside me. Honestly, can't he buy sex like anybody else?'

I smiled wanly at my attempt at a joke, because I knew that stoic women tried and failed at joking, and then I hesitated, as I'd heard frightened women hesitate.

'You cannot say anything to him. I don't want any trouble. I just want what's rightfully mine.'

Kenneth had turned his upper body away; he wanted to get out of there, or even better, disappear.

'I want my home, Kenneth. The home I built for us.'

That last part had sounded better in my head, but I didn't need to worry. Kenneth's demon had sprung to life, and roared. Kenneth wasn't as dumb as he looked. He knew he'd been presented with the opportunity to be a good man. I watched his mind working feverishly. How did a good man act in this situation? Was Baby capable of doing something like that? Had he not been in Baby's shoes before? Was I a crazy sex witch? Kenneth remembered that women couldn't be accused of lying anymore, and Kenneth was remembering each of the times he'd gone home with a woman a decade, or maybe two, younger than him, when they had been blind drunk, limbs amenable.

'That's a very serious accusation, Bibbs.'

I hissed.

'I know it's serious. You know how he drinks,' and to this Kenneth couldn't say anything, because they usually drank together.

'He was just drunk. And maybe he thought I was awake. . .'

I lowered my voice. 'And I woke up and pushed him away.'

Neither of us said anything for a long time. The night's long wake was catching up with me and despite the medication I was tired.

'So,' I insisted, 'can you help me?'

Kenneth thought about how this day could have unfolded in a nicer way, had he slept elsewhere or not answered the door when I rang the bell. He might have cycled down to Reimersholme for a morning swim, and dropped in on Baby on the way home, and Baby wouldn't have asked for anything.

'Yes, of course I'll help you, I just have to. . . I just have to think, I have to sort a few things out, I mean.' The calm kicked in and I smiled at him from the depths of my heart outwards, the knife dislodged. Leaning back.

'Thanks, Kenneth. That warms my heart. I knew I could trust you.'

Kenneth drew his hand away and before he had a chance to change his mind, we were interrupted by a young woman who came up and apologised for interrupting, but. . .

'Yes,' I replied, beaming at her as I had just beamed at Kenneth. 'That's right. Of course it's me, Bibbs.'

My breakfast with Kenneth turned into lunch, then dinner; we ambled through shops, and I bought nothing, but Kenneth bought a gold locket. 'I'm going to put a picture of my daughter in there.' We went to the office and Texas had carried his desk chair onto the pavement. Nothing but moss was growing between the cobblestones. He smoked his e-cig in the stubborn sun, his short-sleeved plaid shirt unbuttoned down his chest, and nestled in his curly chest hair was a gold chain catching the light. Like water droplets, after swimming in Brunnsviken. As if Texas's body was something to caress your way into.

'Mickey said you'd get me a job.'

Texas stalled, reaching for a coin that had fallen out of his pocket and was rolling down the street. So good to see you Kenneth, Texas said. Kenneth said, You too.

'Mickey said you'd help me,' I reiterated. Texas gave me a blank look.

'But he's in LA.'

Kenneth, uncomfortable with even the slightest bit of friction, said:

'Bibbs, but I said I'd help you out.' He said it to help Texas. I thought about pride. Pride doesn't pay. I figured it was smart to show Kenneth my hand. Every card. Show him that they were all worthless.

'All righty,' Texas said, 'see how well that worked out?'

I held back my tears almost all of Sunday; the nearer night drew, the harder it was. While we sitting at the bar at Tranan, after the patio had closed, and Elahe's Ritalin made me more frozen than sharp, they burst out. Tranan's basement was windowless and it was impossible to adjust to the dark even though my pupils were fully dilated, hiding the colour of my eyes. The tears were classic drunk tears, pitiful, unstoppable. 'You deserve better, Bibbs,' Kenneth said, and I wanted to believe him. Instead, I said he didn't understand and buried my face in my hands. Boohoo, I said, thinking that's how crying sounded. Boohoo. Of course he understood. What was there not to understand? But that's how drunk tears are, vain and banal. I stumbled home with Kenneth at my side, fiddling with the lock before he noticed that I was at the wrong door. He followed me in and put me to bed on Elahe's black leather sofa.

In the morning I lay there on the sofa, wary of the slightest movement. Wait, hadn't something bad happened yesterday? The hairband around my wrist burnt and, after I took it off, it left a red ring behind. I tied my hair back. The bad thing was that I had said that Baby had raped me. My insides were so dry they chafed.

'There are different types of kin,' I'd recently said to Baby when he came home early from work to take care of me. I had done my upper lip line and the bruise was keeping me from going out.

'There's cancer kin and heart kin and psycho kin. And I'm psycho kin.'

'And?' he replied.

'And you're psycho kin, too. It's good for the long haul, but messy in the short run.'

My family members lay in dark rooms, gambled away their inheritance, drank until their marriages broke down, and locked themselves in the bathroom, and all our lives we threatened each other with dying if we didn't get our way. But we were fit as fiddles right up until our ninetieth birthdays and then we went gently into the night, surrounded by incredulous family members. Mum would say that she wanted to dig up her father to check that he was really in the grave, his death was that unlikely.

Baby's kin were psycho kin, too, but the kind that acted out. They broke windows with their bare hands, wrung the necks of taxi drivers, got arrested by the police, were unfaithful and didn't bother to come home, and poured pots of freshly boiled spaghetti over their girlfriend's head. In a way this was a bad fit with my flavour of psycho kin, because we tended to fizzle rather than explode, but in a way good because it made me more sympathetic than I could have been had I been of cancer kin. I'd respond with ingratiation to Baby's affirmative anger, as I imagined daughters did with their fathers. Children don't leave their parents, because they don't have anywhere to go, and that's why each pot of spaghetti bound me tighter to my man.

Even if it was best to leave of your own volition, the next best thing was to be left through death following a sudden or prolonged illness, as was often the case in cancer kin or heart kin. Being left was the worst, whatever the kin. In fact never being able to leave your partner was a criterion for being psycho kin, and now I was wondering if I had been wrong about Baby. Imagine if he wasn't psycho kin after all. What if he was blood pressure kin? When I told Kenneth this during our nightcap, he'd listened attentively. Elahe's couch stuck to my skin when I lay on my side, and I remembered that I'd bought something yesterday, a blender. Around the black leather sofa cushions ran an aluminium frame. Where had I left the blender? Kenneth and I hadn't said anything more about the loan, but I'd treated him to more rounds than I usually would as a gesture of goodwill.

In Elahe's kitchen, butter and San Pellegrino were left out on the table. The fridge was ajar and blinking, but had stopped beeping. I shut it.

Falling in love with Baby had meant that I could fall in love with pretty much anyone I met, because now I saw my lover in everyone. That's how potently he inhabited me, and this was one of the more romantic reasons I'd betrayed him, which I'd only done once. It wasn't planned, but a classmate from high school got in touch after clearing out his family home and finding an old diary entry he'd made about me. I was flattered. I didn't know anyone was writing about me back then. My old classmate was married and had recently become a father, but his mother was mentally ill and he needed someone to talk to. We spent hours writing to each other, often talking about a short film he was directing, joking that I should be in it. The film was about a man who sees a woman at the supermarket and asks her out. The twist is that the woman turns out to be his fiancé's sister, whose existence was unknown to the fiancé.

When my old classmate came to Stockholm for the casting, we were going to take a walk through Gamla Stan, just to say hello, but walked back to his hotel and masturbated together because I was in the middle of a herpes outbreak. Before I took off my clothes I answered a message from Baby, asking if he should pick up the dry cleaning. Yes, I wrote. And drop off the yellow one too. Afterwards, my old classmate felt so anxious he deleted his Facebook and I never got a chance to be in the movie. The role we had discussed, that of his wife, would have suited me perfectly.

Did I feel guilty about it? Yes and no. I had never outright promised Baby to be faithful. I'd ask Baby if he'd cheated on me several times a week and made him swear not to, but Baby would never be so bold as to demand such assurances from me.

I took another bottle of water from the fridge, and drank it up. Then I went into the bathroom and ran a bath. The enamel cooled me down and I would go on to fill the tub until it was almost overflowing, and then use my foot to pull out the plug and let the water drain. I'd repeat this procedure two, three times.

Breaking a promise was not something that, in itself, made me feel bad. My conscience operated within other parameters. Every time I told one of my friends what I really thought of Baby, I felt guilty and wrote to them the next day saying I'd exaggerated and that Baby was the best. I also felt guilty about saying that one of his tattoos was ugly, because the way I'd said it was long-winded. Yes, I'd been poking fun at him. Baby hadn't got mad, but had asked what the hell he was supposed to do about it now. I felt guilty about that. But having encouraged an old acquaintance to shoot his load between my butt cheeks wasn't something I thought about often. For one thing, it wasn't planned. Second, Baby was supposed to be above all that. Third, the word 'load' was so inaccurate that it betrayed my classmate more than I'd betrayed Baby.

I got out of the tub. The water gushed down my body and I tracked puddles into the living room to get my phone. With wet fingers, I managed to write to Kenneth. 'Thanks for yesterday. And thank you for your help. When can you make the transfer?' I had decided not to call Baby until the money was in my account.

My cheating on Baby was related to Baby's hometown of Jönköping. I had been to Jönköping many times in the past few years but still felt like a stranger in the city. Baby prized martyrdom, almost ideologically, and this I understood as the legacy of the mountain. A legacy all men in Jönköping contended with. It had to do with the fact that the quarry had shut down, so they weren't able to convert the intractable stone into capital. Instead, they bore those hills like an emotion. Baby, who worked in retail, had never said anything outright, but I was sure he'd rather be working with hills. I was also sure that he considered his profession to be superior to mine. Well hell, even I consider his profession to be superior to mine, I'd joke with the people who asked about Baby's job and didn't have a single follow-up question after he'd muster a reluctant reply. But comparing our professions now, outside the familiar confines of Slipgatan, I realised that this was a lie. I certainly didn't consider Baby's profession to be superior to mine, and I remembered that neither did Baby. It was the reason he'd seduced me and when we first met, Baby's expectations of my life had been impossible. He'd watched television his whole entire life and his profession was conventionally boring. If I'd ever said otherwise, it would have been to soothe his innate sense of inferiority. 'The word for that is "class",' Baby had roared once when I'd called it 'inferiority'.

In and of itself, I thought while folding the blanket that had slid from the couch to the parquet before going back into the bathroom, doing something you hate for as many years as Baby takes a special kind of talent. Like a conviction that after this life, there's another to come. Baby rarely told me that I was good at what I did, but I heard him use both my first and last name when he talked to people we didn't know, to make sure they knew that the woman he was here with was Bibbs-Bibbs, *the* Bibbs.

Fuck the fans were Mickey's words of wisdom for me early on. But Baby's blank, aimless future was irresistible, and my desire to indulge his longing for consumption trumped Mickey's warning. This gloss made Famous Bibbs possible, Bibbs-Bibbs, the one his friends had seen on the cover of a magazine. And Baby felt so flattered that he was allowed to come home with me he didn't notice that the other Bibbs and I didn't resemble each other. When we talked about our lives the next morning, it turned out that his was tinged with a suffering related to social democracy. Baby had two hard-working parents with union memberships and broken backs. The inherent goodness of an aspirational existence was appealing, but not seductive enough for me to want to enjoin myself. I did, however, want this aspiration by my side. I wanted Baby by my side.

Before getting back into the bath, I dried my hands on a towel to make using the phone easier. The noise from the tap calmed my thoughts, but the tub was empty because I had forgotten to replace the plug. Mickey called. He was probably suffering from jet lag. I fussed around before answering.

'Bibbs. There you are.' The line was crisper than yesterday. If I hadn't known he was in the US, I would have thought he was down the street. 'Bibbs, what the hell am I hearing?'

'I don't know, Mickey, what did you hear?'

'How should I put it. . . Of course I understand that it's delicate. I spoke to Kenneth.'

My stomach churned. If Kenneth had gossiped about the money, Mickey would insist it was a bad idea, as I was already in enough debt. 'Kenneth told me about the thing that happened to you.'

Of course Kenneth had gossiped about Baby's rape. Kenneth and Mickey knew each other through me, but even so they kept each other informed about all sorts of shit because there was an unspoken bond between two middle-aged men who had a platonic relationship with a woman. How could I not have taken that into account? Well, because

Kenneth had managed to fool me, that's why, with his horny talk about how sick it was to restrict abortion rights in Poland and because he tipped me off about a podcast with a female host.

'I don't know what you're talking about, Mickey.'

'The thing that happened to you. . . With Baby.'

ON LYING

It's almost impossible to take back a lie, no matter how small. Let's imagine that an acquaintance asks you if you've seen a certain movie. You offer a quick: 'Sure.' That lie, which is insignificant and vain (or ingratiating), is borderline impossible to take back. At no point in the conversation can you say: 'I lied about having seen the film.' To take back a fib is to expose a human being in all their piteousness. Taking back a big lie is easier, because the intention behind a big lie is easier to understand and explain. But that's no picnic either, because you have more at stake. What does a liar look like? Like people do. They're not tucking their hair behind their ears or scratching their noses. The lying liar is the picture of calm because the lie has become part of the liar in a way that holds more truth than anything else.

Besides, had I said to Mickey, while I was in the tub, 'No, I lied, Baby didn't rape me,' I wouldn't have trusted that the truth would have stayed between him and me. Mickey would get it in his head to play the hero and tell Kenneth, or worse, Baby, about my lie. If Baby found out about the lie, he'd forever feel sorry for me and every bad thought he'd ever had might seem true. If Kenneth found out about the lie, there'd be no money, and no apartment, and the outcome would be the same:

Everything bad Baby had ever thought about me might seem true.

'I'd hoped that would stay between me and Kenneth. I don't want it getting out. It's very private.'

'Of course it's private.'

'And if Baby found out, there'd be hell to pay.'

'No, of course, Baby won't find out.' Mickey hesitated.

'That's really brave of you, daring to talk about it. With Kenneth, I mean.'

'Yeah, I needed to get it off my chest. And you were so busy yesterday.'

'Sorry about that. I couldn't have imagined it would be anything like this. But here it is, and well, a lot of people are talking about this stuff. And sharing their experiences and helping others by talking about it.'

I could sense where Mickey was going with this. More than once he'd made jokes about how getting gang-raped could be a career move for me. 'Mickey, I really truly have no desire to talk about this.'

Mickey said he understood. Then we talked about what Mickey wanted to eat, it was night-time where he was and he was hungry, and as I was ending the conversation so I could get ready to shoot a collaboration, he interrupted me. His voice bore witness to what the last few days had been like for him. He had felt young, younger. He didn't need much sleep. His clean-shaven cheeks had acquired a tan. He'd been playing Lana Del Rey's latest album, an artist he'd heard of but hadn't taken the time to listen to, but who he liked, as long as she wasn't being ironic. He'd been thinking of getting a summer place abroad, LA was too far away of course but maybe Lisbon or Palma.

'You know how I feel about exploitation, Bibbs.'

'You like it.'

'Like hell I do.'

'OK, sorry, I thought you liked it.'

'I'm just saying, there's a story here that other people could relate to. Think about it.'

Even though I hated disappointing Mickey, I said I had to go. He wished me luck and said he'd send me the address, even though I assured him that I already had it.

While we were on the phone, I had forgotten that the rape was a lie because the need to protect the lie had got in the way of the fact of the lie. I thought through my and Baby's shared sexual history. Given that we both came from psycho kin, it would be out of the ordinary for him not to have ever committed any abuse. A standstill. The fact was that, after our happy summer, Baby had been borderline castrated (my words) and our lack of sex was the topic of a recurring argument. I'd sulk about it, but tried to hide how I felt behind passive-aggressive seduction attempts. My seductions resembled nagging that began with me pressing myself against his legs while he was still asleep and then putting my hand on his chest. 'Come on,' I'd say, 'come on now.'

For Baby, relationships were a reprieve from the constant demand for sex, and after I'd been rejected for a long period of time, I stopped talking to him. At first I started sending curt replies to his text messages, and when he called out hello upon coming home from work, I didn't return the greeting. Then I stopped talking altogether, lying in our bed at Slipgatan and writing things on my phone as if he weren't there. Sometimes I started crying without saying why. After a few days of silence, he'd cave and we'd sleep together, and I thought he seemed happy afterwards. As if he only needed to be reminded of his desire. After we slept together, it was as if a thick fog lifted and my bad mood seemed to have been over the top, even for me. But Baby's stubborn refusal obliterated me, and my resistance to his resistance became solid granite. Baby couldn't turn the stone. How could I help that? I wrapped myself in a towel. Kenneth and Mickey would never ask Baby about my claim, or force him to talk. That's not how men go about things. Even though I'd recently filled my nasolabial folds, I thought people could sense how deep they ran. My cheeks sagged all the way down to my shoulders.

No one was waiting for me at reception when I arrived at the address Mickey had finally sent, but I had saved the receipt from the taxi. The drive to Åsögatan had been a chore. The jacket I had put on over my big T-shirt was too hot for this weather and the hangover was making my heart clatter. Clutching the lipsticks in my pocket, I swallowed my nausea. I usually did the photography for my collaborations at home but the company had insisted on taking the pictures in their office. I should have asked Mickey what the product was. I was thinking about the money, the money. In the reception area was a company directory and it could be any one of them. Headphones, maybe? Nah, that sounded too good to be true. A schoolchild came out of the elevator. She said, 'Bibbs?' I held out the long receipt that had gone wrinkly in my hands. Reluctantly, she took it.

'You wouldn't happen to have cash for that?'

I'm just an intern, she said. I said give it back. We rode the elevator up three floors.

'Wait here. Someone will come get you soon.'

The intern went away and soon another young woman approached me. 'I'm so glad you're here,' the new woman said, but said 'glad' like she was angry. Follow me. I'm Vanessa. We rode the elevator up another floor. 'Babbs is here,' she said as we got out. I flinched but didn't correct her. Maybe I'd heard wrong. My heart was pounding. Maybe taking the pills with this hangover had been a bad idea. The younger woman glanced at me, my hair still damp from the bath. 'So you have dark hair now?' We entered a disused office landscape with large windows. The trees didn't reach this high. I thought of the last day of the year, of winter. How, when the break-up was over and done with, I would count our hours objectively. Hopefully there would be no snow this year, so that the route up the stairs from Slipgatan to Verkstadsgatan would feel short. The stairs that on a day like this were sheltered by greenery and spilt me out onto a leafy avenue. You shouldn't brush your hair when it's wet, that's why it's tangled. There's one of about 200,000 other rules. The woman wasn't talking to me and I couldn't think of anything to say, either. I was thirsty. I was horny. I missed all the skinny-skinny guys I'd slept with who made my ass feel fantastic. I knew who I was thinking of. Think of something else.

'Excuse me?' the woman said. You don't happen to have any beer? I asked, then said I was happy to be here. Vanessa pointed to an armchair and called me Babbs again. Sit here, Babbs, we'll be back for you soon. No, we don't have any beer. But I can get one of our collagen drinks. Oh, right, energy drinks with collagen. Now I remembered. 'Any Atarax?' For my allergies, I added, but no, none of that either.

I watched her walk away. She was very petite. Stiff white jeans and soft white T-shirt. The trousers cut into her buttocks. Parted them. Kenneth would have freaked out. People came in all sizes and it was one of those things that I thought was cute and moving to think about. Small men were friends with big men. Small men loved big women. Baby loved the way his slim body made my big body feel, as if it were overflowing, and like he had his hands full. I considered sneaking into the bathroom and watching a fat girl get fucked by two thin men. I closed my eyes. Tried to shake off the horny melancholy.

The make-up artist put me in a tall chair and had no idea who I was. I felt sorry for myself, but tried not to let on. 'So, what do you do for a living?' I said: I want you to draw the eyeliner straight, not angled up. My eyes are so close together. She started applying make-up to my skin with a thick brush. 'Such lovely colour, have you been abroad?' Yes, I lied.

'Where?' Sicily with my boyfriend.

She kept applying.

'Vanessa warned me about your hair. You were asked to come with your hair done.' It was hard to ignore her because my phone was out of reach.

'Was it a late one last night? I promise not to tell.' She winked, like in a movie. She looked perky. As if she'd always been perky.

'It was my boyfriend's birthday.' I understand, she said. Maybe she understood. Congratulations to him then. Thank you. Have you been together long? No. Yes. Quite a while.

The make-up sat on top of my skin instead of absorbing and the cream I'd borrowed from Elahe pilled under the product. I used my index fingers to stretch the skin at my temples. This is what I want to look like. She stopped applying make-up. I'll see what I can do but first a little tweeze – she pointed to my moustache. Her long nail glanced my upper lip. My eyes teared up as she plucked.

'Oh no, did that hurt a lot?' I wished I had my phone handy because I would've used it to whack her in the face, I wished I had a cake because then I'd have grabbed her by the hair and smashed her face into it. I was thinking of the fat girl getting fucked by those dicks.

'Sorry, keep this to yourself, but I'm pregnant. That's why I'm extra sensitive.' The make-up girl's eyes softened. 'And here I was thinking you're hungover! Hormone hangover more like it, haha.' We laughed. 'Do you already have children?' 'Nope, this is my first.' 'Well, then double congratulations.' 'Thanks! But it's early days.' She put a hand on my knee. 'I promise not to say anything.' She kept working on me. 'I'm pretty sure I can do your eyes the way you want.'

When Baby and I first got together, I'd decided to let go. To really give in. Time passed but nothing came. All through our happy summer, I worried about Lyme disease in the evenings. Baby thought my liking to be outdoors was lovely. That cunt can die. I can't believe he left me. He can go fuck a thousand whores, but never his own wife. I was thinking about his sex half-hard against my thigh. Nothing to mount. Nothing that could take my weight. My body went between cold and hot at the thought of all the women he'd meet, and I got up halfway. My face had gone grey from the foundation, which didn't match my skin tone.

'I have to pee.' The make-up artist assured me that we were almost done.

I should have made us differently. I shouldn't have told him he's a bad lay, I said that in the kitchen. More than once. The first time, he punched a hole into the wall. Another time he held back tears. Sometimes, to really torture myself, I'd scroll through our conversations just to relive my stupidity. I could argue about anything, any time. This wouldn't have been a problem if Baby didn't function in exactly the same way. I used to tell Baby I was crazy and he didn't agree with that in our first year together. Back then he'd hold me to the best of his ability while I cried with my mouth wide open and my eyes shut. Anxiety frightened Baby to the core. Baby's mother was crazy, so in a way he was used to it, but I knew that being used to something was not the same as being able to handle it. Being used to something means being in it without any resistance, without understanding how to break free.

Today's production was a cheap one, and so there was no wardrobe. A few years ago wardrobe was always part of it. I was reminded of a film about a girl who was about to get

DAYS & DAYS & DAYS

laid by her brother, and when she took off her trousers her thighs had long scars from cutting, which took me out of the story. Those small details were important. Lots of make-up artists forget about scars, for example, like in that film, or about putting make-up on my ears. In the pictures afterwards, they'd be red.

The studio was a corner of the disused office landscape and on the big white wall they had painted a pink square, which would be the backdrop for the image. The photos would be published on the company's Instagram and on my Instagram and the make-up artist was also handling hair and wardrobe. When I told her I hadn't brought any clothes, her friendly face became formal. She turned to Vanessa, the younger woman, and grumbled, 'She didn't bring any clothes,' which was unnecessary because I'd just said the same thing. I guess I was a size 44. Or maybe 46. I didn't think that was very big. No one else would agree. Vanessa said to me: 'Our email said that you should bring at least one change of clothes.' Then she said to the make-up artist, 'Our email said that she should bring at least one change of clothes.'

My agent is in LA, I replied.

'We sent the email directly to you.'

I ran my hand over my face only to remember that I was wearing make-up. I'm sorry, I turned to the make-up artist. She walked off.

'What I'm wearing won't work?' I didn't have a bra on today either. Vanessa said: 'It doesn't matter what you're wearing on your bottom half,' while staring at my breasts. The stare wasn't like Kenneth's. She was weighing them.

'Can't you make a call and have someone bring some clothes over?' What a good idea, I said encouragingly, pretending it was the stylist who had fucked up and not me. I called Texas.

While waiting for Texas, I read the email I had missed. Everyone who was doing a shoot with the drink was listed. I read my name. Besides me, there were two vloggers, and one of them had gone live while getting their ass done. Sometimes I toyed with the idea of doing my ass but wasn't sure if it would pay off. The time that had already gone by was made up of so many lost opportunities, like when I watched the wind blow across the wilder part of Haga and each leaf and each blade of grass sailed through the air on its own. Each leaf was a thing that hadn't happened to me. Among the list of drink personalities was a presenter for *Aftonbladet Morgon* and KK, an ironic poet born in the Nineties. She'd written a poem about seeing me at Riche, by myself, staring at my phone. As if it were proof of something. I wondered what. When I was at my most recognisable, I would whine to my friends while drunk; nowadays I'd talk about the moments when I was recognised in a natural way. Baby was kind and attested that it happened often, and maybe it did, but the recognition had shifted from an exclamation to a question mark.

As of this year, it was eleven years ago. Your cult show, Mickey called it. Before television flatlined and died, there was an energy in the media, as if television were the true internet. A decade later, I realised that it would have been lucrative to have focused more on being a presenter, less on being a participant. Marite said she had tried to tell me as much, but I'd always seen myself as the young poet had, as the person alone at Riche. And that person was unbearable. I was paying Marite so I might as well agree. She was right about one thing: my quality was never about a specific talent I had, I was good at *being*. That said, I only did well on reality TV one time. Besides, I had missed that wave too. Had I started earlier, I could have been the eccentric one, or the sexual one, but now I was there as 'Bibbs', and she was already a public figure. My participation came with a demand for interiority, or a demand to expose more than what I had already exposed (everything), which was hard. I didn't have anything more to give. But I was fat, attractive, and tactless, and women loved me, though not so much that I had their loyalty.

Unlike Mickey, I didn't think I had peaked at MTV. My peak was the credit card commercial, a collaboration I did after my first docusoap but before the cash card commercial, the autumn after the happy summer. 'Docusoap' – it's not called that anymore. On the set of the credit card collab we were served fish for lunch and cold-cold wine and were well-well paid. The stylist had a whole rack of clothes in my size and I got to keep a hat. After that, there was a cultural debate about whether or not I was a feminist, as the general opinion seemed to be that a feminist should not have a credit card. I wasn't reading anything about myself anymore so I don't know who won the debate, but if someone had asked me, I would have said that it was true. I wasn't a feminist. There was no political motivation behind this, I had simply run out of ideals. I felt forlorn. Disappointed. Your actual problem, Baby would have said, is that you've sold out. Sold out what, though? I didn't feel that I was in possession of a true moral superiority and genuine essence that under no circumstance could be compromised. Such reasoning was far too vain. When I read my name, it meant nothing to me. I had tried to explain all this in my podcast 'Call Bibbs' or 'Call Bibbi' or 'Talk to Bebbe' or whatever the hell it was called. I'm not here because of a popular vote, I would have said. I'm not a local politician. I'm not accountable to anyone. Then I was accused of, well, I don't remember now, but I would have agreed on principle. I was fucking awful. There were other jobs. A person doesn't have to sell out. But everything had seemed so brilliant.

When Texas finally arrived at the shoot with four tops from a brand I'd worked with a year or two ago, we were already an hour into overtime. The battery on my phone was low. I hadn't washed my hands. The tops he had brought were cheap but were in a wrap style that everyone agreed suited my body type. 'Were there no bras?' I asked, annoyed, because I had told him to bring one. He had already accepted a Red Bull. The can hissed when he cracked it open. 'No, I came straight from the office.' The make-up artist's mouth was set in a line.

'Is he on payroll?' I didn't answer.

'Come on, I'll tape your breasts, I have duct tape in my kit.'

I hadn't taken my clothes off in front of anyone except Baby in a very long time and as I pulled the T-shirt over my head I felt small. Baby always said: 'You're so lovely,' when I took my clothes off. The make-up girl said she could tell I was pregnant, before she attached the tape under one breast and stretched the tape around my neck, and cut the strip. The hair on my neck got stuck and I teared up again, but not because it hurt. I was thinking about the money. The memory of happiness was a wisp of smoke. Then she fastened the tape under my other breast and pulled it up towards my neck. She fiddled for a while to get the breasts even until she was finally satisfied and cut the strip. There, that should look good. I put my wrap top on and tied its belt around my waist. In the mirror I could see that it did look good. 'You should have them done as a treat for yourself after you give birth, I did,' she said. 'If all goes to plan.'

The podcast had been an attempt to recreate the magic I'd achieved with my blog, but it was a mistake, I knew that on the day I agreed to do it. But several streaming services were trying to compete with Apple and they were throwing money around. Unfortunately, the big money was hard to come by and I had a chewing gum sponsor who paid per stream. The ad sales rep said it was hard to find sponsors because my brand and the podcast's mission were unclear. The podcast's mission, I'd said, was to sell ads. Sorry, but that's not how it works, the salesman said (a guy who did jujutsu). 'Would have been easier if you had kids,' he said while biting into an apple. The apple looked irresistible in his large hand. 'Talk to Bibbs' – that's what it was called, and the concept was that anyone could leave a message on an answering machine about what was in their heart. I'd answer their questions on the podcast with my signature tactlessness. Most questions had to do with the TV shows I'd done in recent years and how to reboot your life, as it turned out that my brand was my yo-yoing weight and being a has-been, but like as a joke. Some questions were about the blog. No one, almost no one, remembered my show on MTV. Mainly, too few questions came in. I asked my friends, my mother, and Baby to leave a message on the answering machine. Baby kept forgetting. After eighteen episodes, we called it quits, and by then he still hadn't asked a single question.

I was glad my breasts were in place and went into the studio. I asked who was going to shoot and the make-up artist said, 'Me.' God help me, I thought, and found a spot amidst the shaggy furniture. I was supposed to be drinking soda in a girl's bedroom and the intern put a basket of the collagen drink on the table in front of me. The cans were not refrigerated. Texas waved at me from the back of the room. My tears stung. It felt like I loved him.

'The next personality will be getting here soon, so—' Vanessa said.

'What's your job again?' I interrupted.

'Marketing,' she said, and I knew she'd never held anyone in the night, at knifepoint, and no matter how carefully I'd try to explain, she wouldn't understand. Her hair looked like feathers and she was wearing heeled boots in sandal weather. Her jeans cut not only into her buttocks, but into her vulva too.

'And what am I?' She took a breath.

'A brand ambassador.' I took a can from the basket and sat down on the stool, which was next to a bright-pink table and covered with a large cushion. The table was sloppily painted.

'It's important for us to feature personalities of all sizes,' Vanessa continued. I opened the can.

'I'm a presenter,' I said, 'but you're probably too young to have seen me.'

'Drink it,' shouted the make-up artist behind the camera. The lights were so bright they made my scalp itch.

'Your hand is shaking, put it down,' shouted the make-up artist. I put the can down.

'Is drinking really a good look?'

'It hides your double chin,' the make-up artist said, and looked up from behind the camera.

'The fact that you're older is just a bonus, so it doesn't matter about the make-up,' the woman continued.

'What about the make-up?' Texas asked from the wings.

'I'm not older. Why am I supposed to look older?'

'We booked you because you're you.' Everybody's mouth was smiling, psychotically, and I watched their heads separate from their bodies, like I had watched each leaf on its own in the untended part of Haga. The intern's phone rang and she ran out of the studio to answer it and soon came running back.

'Bianca's on her way.'

Both women got jumpy. The intern tugged at her short sundress and I glimpsed her panties underneath. I thought about the fabric stretching across her pubic mound.

'Your hair looks great, natural.' My face was itchy from the make-up and the Ritalin. I held you in the night at knife-point, I thought, and then I thought about the money. It was nerve-wracking sleeping with the knife. I wanted it to be worth something.

'Don't tense the corners of your mouth like that.' I took a sip of the drink and spat it back out.

Every bad decision is related to invoicing, I told Texas as he tried to tear the duct tape off my back inside the accessible toilet that served as a dressing room. He was shaky, too. I told him to stop. The younger woman came in.

'In your post write that you noticed a change in your cellulite, in particular, and we'll email you times for when to publish it.' I nodded and started looking for my things so the woman would leave.

'You didn't bring anything with you,' said the make-up artist who had also walked in, 'but you're the only one who brought someone.' The extensions sewn into her blunt-cut hair were a lighter shade of brown than her real hair, and I thought of a neighbour who'd attached her cousin's cut-off hair to her own with a glue gun. Should I tell that story? I thought, but then I remembered my travel expenses.

'You don't happen to have cash for my taxi receipt?'

The women just blinked at me. Texas held out his hand to say goodbye and soon we were down on the street. Morning had turned into afternoon. I was hungry, tired and thirsty. I was older. I checked my phone for the hundredth time. No one had got in touch. Not even Kenneth to confirm the money transfer. I was thinking about the money.

Texas ordered for both of us. The wall-to-wall carpeting made it hard to breathe, I thought, but I didn't feel like complaining. There was nothing else to complain about. Everything I was afraid of had already happened. Texas had taken me to Casino Cosmopol to cheer me up and promised to pick up the tab. On the bar was Texas's hat, which had left red marks at his temples. There was something familiar in his manner, not to me but to the world. A kindness in the deep furrows of his brow that disarmed strangers. As a reflex I felt along my wrist to take off the hair tie, but it wasn't there. I asked about the hat and he answered, both of us bothered by the fact of spending time together when Mickey wasn't about to join us. Bibbs, he said. You know I'm always worried about you. I see things differently from Mickey, he thinks you're so tough.

I looked at the phone. If anyone wanted me, I was available.

'Mickey asked me to check in with you,' Texas said after waiting in vain for me to put my phone down. I didn't know how I felt about him and Mickey, but on the way to the casino, after I'd appeased my hangover with a 7-Eleven hot dog, the love I'd felt for him in the studio had evened out. The love was no more than hunger, and the meat had burnt the roof of my mouth and I was prodding the blister with my tongue. I wondered what Mickey and Texas thought about me, even though I knew what they thought of women in general: women were either ugly or attractive. Baby never said it outright, but I knew he saw the world in the same way. Early in our relationship he'd told me that one of my female acquaintances looked like a pig and I'd been shocked by his heartfelt disdain, but now I thought: 'So what?' Didn't we all see the world that way, in terms of pigs and foxes. The soda in the drink was not well carbonated, but the taste of vodka was soothing. The lights flashed in the machines and flickered in the blackness of Texas's eyes. Texas was talking as if he were there with a different person. All I wanted was for Baby to love me, but inside I hesitated. No, that's not all I wanted. Oh, so Texas had stopped talking.

'Earth to Bibbs?' I told him that I was going out for a smoke and asked for a cigarette. He slowly pulled one out of his pack and held it in his hand to hold my attention.

'Baby seemed to care about you so much. But "still waters", I suppose.'

A man missing his left canine was walking behind me down the stairs. Kungsgatan was less busy than usual and beggars weren't allowed outside the casino. The gap-toothed man had a plastic bag in one hand and looked like he spent too much time in one room. He said something in Russian and I smiled to show that I didn't understand.

'That means "do you have a light?" But it's not my language either.'

I lit his cigarette like a gentleman. He was dressed in a sporty beige jacket from the Eighties and underneath the jacket was a way-too-big polo shirt. We smoked together and I didn't inhale and let the smoke flow elegantly out of my nose. The casino guard shouted for us to stand further from the entrance and we walked down the street towards the 7-Eleven, where the outcasts were allowed to sit with their broken bags. The night, unlike the day, offered the possibility of surprise, and it was this possibility that drew me out even after I got to know all the faces and the names that went with them. The man before me didn't look like he had potential and probably nothing would happen, but it might. . . My days with Baby were something else. They were a promise of something predictable and the predictability was an attempt to instil order.

'I've lost my Baby,' I told the man.

'Just be glad you had something to lose in the first place. I haven't had a woman in years, because I'm neither macho nor cold.'

No woman wants a cold man, I promised.

'Sometimes I say to women, "Let's go to my place and mess around and see where it takes us," but women expect more. Do you have any vices, by the way?'

'Well, I do smoke.'

'Well, not me,' he replied, having now smoked the whole cigarette without once taking it out of his mouth. 'But I like going to the casino because I like the uncertainty. Sometimes I walk out of there with empty pockets thinking: So how am I going to feed myself today? But yeah, I like the insecurity.' He searched for a word. 'No, I mean the uncertainty.' He searched for another word.

'No, the insecurity too. Come on, it's time to let me win!' he shouted. 'If I win, may I invite you on a trip to Moscow? I want to walk across Red Square with you on my arm.'

I was flattered that someone still wanted to seduce me, but before I could answer, Elahe called, and I excused myself.

'Did you put the glass recycling outside the garbage room? A neighbour got in touch.'

Her sober voice tore through the twilight enchantment.

'No, which glass recycling, I didn't put anything anywhere.'

'So you don't sort the trash?'

'Elahe, I have to go, talking on the phone isn't allowed at the casino.'

'The casino? What are you doing there?'

'I'm going to gamble a little with Texas.'

'With Texas?'

'Elahe, I really have to go now, thanks for calling about sorting the trash.'

When I turned around to continue the conversation, my gap-mouthed friend was gone. He'd been celebrating yesterday, he'd said, at home in front of the TV. Celebrating what, I'd asked and noticed his scarred skin. So typical for a Swedish girl not to know. Under his eyes were big blackheads that looked like they were being squeezed out by the movements of his face. His eyelashes were like mink. Sure, I said. I guess it's a bit typical. Tito was my president, he added, with a longing that revealed a hole more familiar to me than Texas's heat. 'But I was always too lonely to join in,' he said quickly, eager to be honest.

The man's cigarette butt was smouldering on the ground and I kicked it. I thought, it doesn't matter that loneliness is hard. Harsh. How to explain it? Like a thing that's twisted, but much bigger than a thing. Nonetheless it's stuck, as if it didn't belong there. That's why I think about the thing itself, and not, for example, the condition. Loneliness is forced on you. Congenital, yet you try to fight it. The more you wriggle, the more stuck it gets. Outside the hotel across the street, I spotted someone I knew. But the cars on the road kept me from shouting hello. Like this man, I also felt drawn to insecurity. No, I mean uncertainty. His palpable melancholy ran like a cold chill down my spine, or maybe it was something chemical. The red light turned green, then red again. Although we had got on well, I hung back. To avoid catching up with him. I wasn't superstitious, but such deep-going bad luck, like a body made up of its failings, could easily become contagious.

Night arrived and with it the insight that we had been drinking more than we had gambled at the casino. Texas was on his way and I was considering saying it like it was, before he left, that Baby had surely raped somebody. Just not me. The lie seemed ridiculous after the long day, like a joke. Jokes could be taken back, and it was understood that jokes contained a measure of truth, however scandalous they were. Whereas a lie was thought to be the only thing in the world without a single grain of truth in it.

Texas droned on about Mickey and how Mickey thought I should write about what had happened with Baby. Don't tell him I said anything, he said, but Mickey said that you need all the help you can get. I asked what Mickey was doing in LA, but Texas didn't hear me. Don't feel bad about today, he said again. The alcohol made Texas look tanned, and he was holding his hat in his hands. Don't feel bad about today, you did your best. I thanked him and kissed Texas goodbye on the cheek, but I decided to stay.

The chairs at the casino were occupied by people with nothing to do but kill time. Between the rows of one-armed bandits, I looked for the man I'd been smoking with, but my companion was nowhere to be found. Maybe he'd won and swept another laughing woman along with him. The casino didn't feel like a place for money, not like a place where it would somehow appear on its own, in some perverse way, like at Elahe's or Kenneth's house. In the casino it didn't appear, it disappeared. There, the dough was sucked into an invisible centrifuge. It was almost ten o'clock and a large group of young men had entered the casino, rowdy and tipsy. They were celebrating something. Whatever there was to celebrate. The money centrifuge sucked my intestines up to my throat, that's how strong it was. There was no point in gambling because on a day like this any money you took out of your pocket would stay outside your pocket. Days were predetermined, as I had always known and later had confirmed by Marite. Days were set about a thousand years before they took place. Humankind's challenge was to surrender to the will of the day, while putting up enough resistance for the day to contend with. Marite often laid the cards out in front of me on the round pine kitchen table and spoke to me without once looking down at them. 'You have to put up some resistance too, Bibbs.'

I went into the bathroom to do a mirror check and found that those three lipsticks were still in the pocket of my green military jacket. Even though I had upwards of fifty lipsticks, it felt like each lipstick was the last of its kind as less and less stuff was being sent to me. When the packages from companies started waning, I felt stressed at first because I thought my cost of living would go up. But none of the things that stopped showing up seemed so essential that I felt compelled to pay for them myself. When there was something I really wanted, I could send an email asking for it, and sometimes (if I was afraid of getting a 'no') I'd use an address I'd set up in another name. 'Hi, I work for Bibbs,' I would write, as a greeting. I didn't miss the things, but I did miss being invited to truly lavish events. The casino was a reminder that glamour isn't where you think it might be and the casino was not like the idea of a casino. But it was cool inside, like at the cinema. Some people make going to events their job, Elahe used to say when I'd been to an event, and I'd say well what's wrong with that? Leave morality to those who need it, I joked.

'Yes, and you need it, Bibbs,' Elahe would reply.

Elahe could talk for hours about whose actions were right or wrong and who had not kept their promises. I was more cautious about speaking out on such matters, because I had a sense that everything I was accused of was true. But I didn't know how this made me a worse person than Elahe. 'Elahe,' I'd said one afternoon as we were walking to Hötorget to fix my smartphone screen. 'We're all convinced of certain lies. And those lies are truer than anything. More true than the truth itself.' Even if the win, like the loss, had long since been written into the day, I would never have been a gambler. My luck was spread out instead of, as for some people, being concentrated in one or two days a year, which was one of the bigger reasons why Slipgatan had to be mine. I'd been buying my weekly EuroJackpot ticket in a shop close to home for a while and when I needed something to calm my mind I'd think of the woman in central Sweden who'd won 155 million. Surely, like me, she was a woman without a specific talent.

'Isn't all of Europe playing that?' Elahe had asked as she accompanied me to the tobacconist's before we went to Hötorget for the phone. The tobacco shop was on the Reimersholme side of the short bridge that ran between Slipgatan and Reimersholme Island.

'Yeah and that's why the pay-out is so big.'

'Is it even worth it? The odds must be terrible?'

Here was the difference between us. Of course the odds were terrible, that was the whole point of playing the EuroJackpot. Terrible odds not only made the potential pay-out bigger, but also more deserved and desirable. 'There's a saying, Elahe. "You haven't got a shot, so take one anyway!"'

No, Bibbs, you most certainly do not have a shot. But you can't not take one. That was the time Elahe bought me a licorice pipe, because I asked her to, as well as a scratch card, and after we left the store we sat on a bench on Söder Mälarstrand. 'Do you play the same numbers each time?'

'Yes, of course. For the peace of mind. I play my numbers every other week, in between I play a different set. And you always have to play your numbers in the same shop so as to not lose there unnecessarily.'

Right after I moved into Slipgatan and hadn't yet quit smoking, the tobacco shop was worse for wear, bordering on down-for-the-count, the dairy products were expired and cigarette cartons were in large net baskets in front of the cash register. The man who ran the shop was not happy with his profession and spent his time on his phone watching cars overtake each other on a racetrack, putting no effort into creating a nice customer experience. I used to sneak a bill out of Baby's pocket while he was in the shower and cross the small bridge to buy a licorice pipe and two loose cigarettes. Fancy seeing you here! I'd joke each time I saw the owner and he'd grunt in reply, not looking up from his screen. The joke was that he couldn't go anywhere.

Last August, I went down to buy the day's ticket and found a civil servant standing behind the counter, so close to the owner that at first I thought they were hugging. The civil servant was speaking earnestly to the owner, who was twenty years older than the ruddy man, and it surfaced that the owner's curly-haired head had known more headaches than the young striver ever would. The owner was crying. I felt embarrassed. Or ill at ease – men crying always make me ill at ease. When I'd complain to Baby about him not crying enough, it was my way of saying: 'That's enough crying.' Men who cried were unreliable and weak, and crushingly beautiful. Men who cried always got their way. I stood there awhile, waiting for the civil servant and the tobacconist to let me buy what I'd come to buy, but I was a ghost or less than a ghost, something entirely without presence. Finally I gave up and left with my errand unfinished, and it would be a long time before I returned. Not because of the poor service, although that would have been reason enough, but because I felt ashamed on behalf of the man.

Three months after I saw the shopkeeper crying, I got tired of walking all the way to Hornstull for my cigarettes and went back to the miserable shop. The second I walked in, I noticed a massive difference. I was hit by the smell of new plastic and the walls were lined with slender, white shelves full of cigarette cartons and dry goods that I later discovered were arranged alphabetically. The floor was a glossy black-and-white chequerboard pattern, and behind the counter glowed a large aquarium empty of fish. Ocean sounds streamed from the white speakers mounted on the wall. Without acknowledging the store's transformation, I asked for the usual, and as I took my change I asked:

'So it's a concept store now?'

The owner looked at me, aware that I'd seen him cry, and this was a man who didn't even cry in front of his wife.

'Concept, sure.' And then, in a conciliatory tone, he asked:

'How about a EuroJackpot ticket?' And that's how I started playing. The shop was as important to me as Slipgatan was, as I'd never before resolved a conflict so smoothly and with mutual respect. I noticed his thumbs were as flat as five-kronor coins as he handed me my first ticket as a gift. A gift that was a clear vision. Like icy water. A daydream that cost only 25 kronor and lasted all week, a fantasy of the simple life with money without the simple life demanding everything in return. The next week arrived with a new shot at winning.

Best of all, the EuroJackpot was more than a dream. The prize could become a reality, as long as I crossed that bridge every seventh day. But I had to go to that shop and no other. You can't confuse luck when luck, as it is for me, is distributed evenly throughout the year and not concentrated in a single day.

My lipstick was on, and I went back into the casino. Unlike the EuroJackpot, where the dream was suggestively distant, here the dream was manically present and manic wishful thinking has a tendency to take up so much space that it displaces personality. A poker tournament had begun on the second floor and the bar was empty, except for a man who had taken off his jacket and hung it over the back of his chair. He was a remarkably ordinary man. His mouth was neither full nor thin. His eyes were neither bright nor tired. Nose neither large nor small, hair neither grey nor brown.

'I'll have a vodka soda, please.'

The man didn't react at first, but when I said 'please' a second time, he turned mechanically toward the bar and ordered one for me. The bartender sprayed the soda out of a hose, and we watched her.

'Vodka soda is a perfect drink.'

'Here you go.'

'Was it expensive enough to warrant my gratitude?' I said, suddenly happy to be talking to someone who didn't know me at all.

'I've seen you on TV,' the man replied, 'or were we neighbours once?'

'Where do you live?'

'Nearby, on Valhallavägen.'

'Then we must be neighbours.'

I had the look of a person who'd had a long day, and it piqued the man's interest.

'I don't believe you,' the man replied.

'The only thing that isn't perfect about a vodka soda is that it runs out so quickly.'

The man turned to the bar again and ordered another vodka soda and a Pepsi Max.

'Do you think I need a soda?'

'It's for me.'

'You're right, we're not neighbours. You've seen me on TV.'

'I knew it! I'm sorry, but which show?'

'I'm a creator. You've probably seen me being interviewed somewhere.'

The man pretended to think.

'Creator, what does that mean you do?'

'What do you do?'

'Oh, I work in HR.'

The man straightened up and I tried to guess how tall he was.

'Now I know where I recognise you from. You were in that TV show a few years ago. Where they eat dinner.'

I finished my second drink. The man asked about the participants in the show and told me what he thought of each one. He didn't like any of the women, especially the one with the backpack. People with backpacks think they've got the whole world in their bag, he said.

'How much did you all get paid for that? 50,000 an episode?'

I laughed. Try ten.

'Ten!'

'So, does your wife also live on Valhallavägen?'

The man laughed, slightly embarrassed.

'Nope, she lives in Norrköping. I work here during the week.'

'So what did you think of me?'

I could sense when money was approaching. When I was younger, all I had to do was think about it hard enough and it would show up.

'Go on, you had an opinion about everyone else. What did you think of me? What did you say to your wife back home in Norrköping?' The man twirled the bottom of the glass bottle around on the shiny counter.

'My wife. . .' Go on, I goaded him, you nerd.

'My wife didn't think you knew how to dress for your body type.'

'And what did you say?'

'I agreed. But—'

'But—'

'But really I thought—'

The man coughed.

'I'm sorry, it's so dry in here.'

'What did you think?'

'I thought you were. . . cool. With your body. Ample.'

'Were you watching when we went swimming, in the lake?'

'Yes.'

'Is that when you thought I was ample.'

'Yes.'

'Did you think about my pussy?'

When I mentioned my pussy, his bland face turned boyish.

'Are you thinking about my pussy now, now that I've asked?'

The man coughed again. He smelt of booze.

'Do you know what the word "gorge" refers to in Greek mythology?' I asked in a low voice.

As he shook his head, he sighed deeply, and, besides the wine and liquor, he smelt of orange.

'Chaos,' I said.

The man picked up the glass next to the Pepsi and set it back down.

'And do you know what my pussy is called?'

He wasn't breathing.

'The Gorge.'

We sat in silence until he broke it.

'What's your name, again? Sorry I know it, of course, but—'

My slides slapped my heels as I slid off my chair and moved closer to him. I was standing so close my lips grazed his stubble.

'Bibbs.'

I heard his heart pounding and thought about listening to Baby's heart beating when I lay awake at night before I had the thought of the EuroJackpot prize to keep me company. My head felt heavy as it rested on Baby, but his sternum supported me. As I moved my face away from the man's ear to meet his gaze, I placed my hand on his thigh.

'Bibbs,' the man repeated and wrapped his arm around my waist.

'Bibbs,' I said, as if the name were bouncing between two trees.

The man's apartment was haphazardly furnished and all he had to offer me was wine from a small screw-top bottle. He had bought it on the train, but hadn't finished it, he told me, and I asked for a glass of water. I was drunk and while he waited for the water in the tap to get cold, I sat down on the sofa bed. My jacket was on the seat beside me like another guest. The apartment made a lonely impression and filled me with the same kind of anxiety as twilight in March. Before the sky turned apricot and still made all the rooms dusky in the afternoon. I stuffed my hand down my tights and pulled my panties to one side. I'd been wet all day.

The man came back and threw himself on top of me before I could say anything; his kisses were heated and wet, as if he were playing catch-up. I saw the glass of water he had placed on the table and it called to me under the crush of his warm body.

'What did you say?'

'I said you're bound to be disappointed,' he repeated, undoing his belt, 'you're probably used to bigger ones.'

'I'm a bit short on cash.' The man had pulled up my big T-shirt and put it around my neck, and I wondered where I had left the plastic bag with the new wrap top. Instead of asking about the money, he tugged at my breasts, then let go, suddenly uninterested. He started kissing my collarbones, my stomach, and grabbing my rolls of fat.

'I'm short on cash,' I repeated as he was going back for my nipple. The man grunted to indicate that I should lift my butt, so he could get my tights off. The scent of my pussy filled the space between us as he pulled my tights past my thighs and he sniffed his way down my stomach, past the happy trail and put his bland nose over my pubic mound. The hair curling under the fabric of my panties made it look soft. He was still dressed and I didn't want to see him naked. The man, who was now between my legs, took a deep inhale of my scent.

'Damn, you smell good.' I snapped my thighs shut.

'I need money,' and he stopped. I knew his type. The type who always eats pussy with one eye on the woman's face, because he couldn't keep going without constant reassurances. He was the type who, after the woman had come, looked up with a glazed mouth and asked, 'Was it good for you?' before she had time to sense whether it really was good or more like scratching a mosquito bite, equal parts satisfying, necessary, and unimaginative.

'Why are you saying that? Or why are you bringing it up now?'

'Well, it seems like you want to fuck me, and I need money. So maybe you can help with the money part?' The glass of water looked cool, like grace.

'You're saying you want to sell me sex?'

'I'm just telling it like it is: you want to fuck me and I need money.'

'But aren't you on TV?'

'I told you what it paid.'

The man slipped a finger under my panties.

'It feels like you want to fuck me?'

I pulled up my tights and excused myself. Before the man could respond, I had walked into the bathroom. The bathroom was smaller than Nina's. I test-flushed the toilet and in the mirror my lipstick was like a rosy shadow around my mouth, across my chin. What did sex pay? My phone was still out in the living room so I couldn't google it. 1,500 maybe? But I was famous and could probably charge more. Each day was predetermined a thousand years before, I reminded myself. Marite's cards neatly fanned out on the pine table and a warmth between us that resembled care. 'This one means ego death,' she said of every other card, and I knew it was Marite's wish for the cards, not the cards' wish for me.

When I came back out into the living room, the man had taken off his trousers and folded them neatly. He was wearing black boxers and black socks pulled up over his hairy ankles. His calves and thighs looked toned. His shirt was still buttoned to the collar and he was sitting on the sofa, elbows on his thighs and hands clasped as if in prayer. Before I could say anything, the man said: OK.

'OK what?'

'OK you can have some money. But not because I'm

buying sex from you. But because I want to give you money. And after that – a separate event that has nothing to do with the first one – I want to have sex with you. Does that sound good?' I nodded.

'2,000?'

4,000, I said. Four? the man said. No whore at Casino Cosmopol costs that much and I said, no, but I'm not a whore from Casino Cosmopol, you said yourself: I'm on TV.

'2,500, then?' I said: Three, but then you can't put your dick in me, you can eat me out and finger me and then we'll jerk off together side-by-side until we both come. He reminded me of Kenneth, if Kenneth had never moved to Stockholm. We masturbated together and he ate me out for a long time, all the while with one eye on me, as predicted. Finally, I came so hard that I let out an honest 'Fuck'. Baby was bad at giving oral sex because oral sex is about daring to make decisions and then following through with them, and Baby was a cowardly man who second-guessed himself. Before we fell asleep in each other's older arms, the man made a transfer, but this has nothing to do with our mutual masturbation, he said, and I said mhm, really couldn't care less.

On Investments

When it came time to sort the money out, I thought about all the money I wanted back. The hand blender almost made the cut. A trainer who told me I had to lose 9 kilos for my knees' sake and who later said, 'A horse knows no age' when I told him how old I was — that was an expense I regretted. I regretted every lunch at a restaurant, because lunch as a meal was more about sustenance than pleasure and you might as well be treated to it. The happy summer, when I was at my skinniest, I wanted to get even skinnier and had a fat-freezing treatment. I regretted that. When I dyed my hair red and it brought out the red in my face and drew attention to the purple and red webbing of broken blood vessels across my cheeks. I want a refund. I regretted removing the blood vessels, which returned, and I regretted removing a tattoo, and I regretted getting the tattoo. That was 25,000 right there. The fillers in my marionette lines somehow made me look like a bear. Was that a good thing? I'd bought two iPads. Why? After lunch, I'd usually buy a smoothie. Unnecessary sugar. All the food I bought was unnecessary sugar. All the late fees on overdue bills annoyed me and all the bills, in general. All the rent I paid. It felt like burning cash. All the trips and especially all the mis-booked flights. All the periodicals and dinners and friends and bus tickets. All the shoes dresses shorts hats drugs. All the drinks. I regretted it all. Except the Americanos. The Americanos I loved.

On Tuesday morning, I left the ordinary man to his fate. We would not meet again, even though we did get a good night's sleep together. When I woke up around eleven and saw the stranger next to me, I realised something that should already have been clear to me. That this had been a bit twisted. Outside, a family walked by and the father screamed: 'Hey, stand still!' Vasastan was on the border of Östermalm and I couldn't see the sky from the narrow bed, but sunlight was being reflected onto us by a windowpane on the building across the street. Someone cracked open a window. The man's eyelids were tense, revealing that he wasn't really sleeping anymore. The absence of Baby's sincere attraction to routine had put me off my game, and I travelled back to Slipgatan as if in a daze. From the street I could see that the kitchen light was on, which was unlike him. Naively, I figured that, like me, he was upset about the separation and was allowing tiny catastrophes to happen. I watched Baby walk around the room. Every cell in my body knew him, which must mean he knew me, too, and if I punched in the code and walked up the stairs and opened the door as if nothing had happened, he'd probably go along with it. My shirt smelt strongly of the man's aftershave and awakened in me a sense of well-being that I wanted to bury. I wasn't going to tell Baby that I'd be buying him dinner tonight, like no big deal. I checked my phone. No one had got in touch. Kenneth hadn't sent any money. I understood what Marite meant, that even the things we didn't say could have meaning. Kenneth was saying something. The question was what? Like all unfamiliar smells, the aftershave took hold of me again, but it already belonged to a different life. That life was not how I was going to win my darling back, and the important thing, I reminded myself, was to come to Baby not as myself, but with what I was willing to sacrifice.

And on Tuesday, with a hook in my heart attached to a line connected to his heart, I was still willing to sacrifice everything. The night had reminded me of something that I, in my privilege, had been able to forget. . . Although night and day followed upon each other, each like the reflection of the other, they had very little to do with each other. I had battled to get out of the night, into the day. I didn't have the time or resources to do anything but keep holding on. I was turning forty next year. That's when a person has no business being out at night, as I used to say about people my age when I was a different age. But the years had gone by faster than I'd imagined they would, of course. Just like they say they do. Much faster.

After I'd said goodbye to my ordinary lover, I went down the street and bought roses for 600, and in the taxi to Slipgatan,

I'd been thinking about what I had left to give. I could stop watching my videos, if that's what he wanted, or start pod-casting again. The taxi driver wished me good luck before I slammed the door. Baby saw no difference between expensive flowers and flowers from the grocery store, but I'd tell him how much they cost anyway. Whenever he accepted my gifts, I'd tell him how much they had cost, however much I didn't want to. Please accept these roses, I'd say when he opened the door, they're a sign of my unfailing love and loy-alty, and then I would say two lines we'd said to each other so often that we said them in our sleep, our backs touching.

'I'm sorry, take me back.'

'I'm sorry, don't leave me.'

Sometimes I'd turn to him and see scratch marks across his back that were longer than his legs. I'd gently follow the scraped skin with my index finger, and in the dark he'd ask me if I was going to leave him, and I always said no. I always, always said no. No is the only answer to that question. That morning outside Slipgatan, after I'd spent the night with a stranger, I was filled with the conviction that if one person feels something very strongly, then other people feel the same way. This separation was painful, I understand now, and the anguish so overwhelming that I wished it had been shared. In case he asked me what I was apologising for, I would say: 'For whatever you want. I'm apologising for everything.' I would tell him about the videos, and I would promise to start work-ing more seriously again. Lately, I'd mostly been watching clips of men having sex with silicone dolls, I could tell him that. Nobody was coming to harm. No women were harmed in the making, and Baby hated it when women were being harmed. I could stop pressing myself against him at night, I could cry or not cry, whichever he wanted. I would never feel lonely again, or imagine that the world was a black hole in which I lay paralysed, in anticipation of that other black hole: death. I would never again punch the building door or throw my phone to the ground, or hurl a cup against the wall.

I promise to never _____ again, and he'd get to choose how to fill the blank space.

Baby turned off the lights in the kitchen and disappeared from the window, but soon reappeared by the sink. I was standing across the street, but it was a narrow street, cramped between the buildings. Quiet at this time. Maybe he saw me but didn't believe his eyes. He opened the fridge and I knew he was going to take the oat milk out and fill his cup. The flowers were in my arms and I started walking towards the entrance. If he saw me now, I'd look like a dream woman. But then something strange happened that I didn't quite understand. Another body entered the kitchen, a short body with long hair. I couldn't see the face. Baby turned to the body, apparently not taken aback by the fact that a stranger was in our home, and the mouths of their two heads met. Before I could see anything more, I took a sharp left and quickly made my way up Högalidsgatan.

Baby II

Baby's dad beat Baby as a teenager and Baby blamed himself because he was bad at school and didn't have a weekend job. I used to contradict him, but when Baby started turning his fits of rage on me, I understood his reasoning, because I understood the anger via our internal logic. Rage was not something that belonged to, or came from, Baby alone, but something that belonged to our relationship and the atmosphere we created together. Besides, he didn't really hit me. He often threw things at me or after me, and would land a punch to one side of me, but never on me. Sometimes he'd throw a punch at my face, but stop his fist right before it made impact with my nose, his knuckles grazing its tip. Once he grabbed me so hard by the arms that bruises appeared the next day, shaking me while shouting at me to get out of the way. Reflexively, I'd given his chest a big shove and said, 'Go on and hit me, you fucking pussy.' I'd said it with complete calm. Go on and hit me. The way my first boyfriend had taught me to say it, in the weeks he spent training me on how to ask him to hit me during sex. It was important not to disrupt the fiction, for it to sound heartfelt and in the beginning he had felt guilty about hitting me without my asking him to. So we practised and I managed it, metabolised the lie until it finally sounded true and then many years later when I said the same thing to Baby I said it with conviction.

When I would still discuss Baby's temper with her, Elahe used to respond with a story about how her husband had once got mad and hit the table so hard the candle fell out of its candlestick. Then Elahe had made it clear that such behaviour was unacceptable and he must never do it again, whereupon he apologised and never did it again. This, Elahe said, was something Bibbs should make Baby understand. But, it was impossible to make someone else understand something you understood intuitively. I could make no argument for why Baby shouldn't act the way he did; this was somatic knowledge that couldn't be transferred to him. A deep intention, and the closest I came to contact with the other side, that Marite talked about. It was easy for Baby to get angry with me, because I could take one look at a person and see what they least wanted to hear about themselves, and then I tell it like it is. My bad sides were crystal clear, but what I was good at was harder to glean, more diffuse.

We spoke two different languages, Baby and I, or maybe our challenge was that Baby encountered me every morning as if for the very first time and couldn't remember the things he'd done to frighten me. As if the romantic promise of never tiring of me had global amnesia as its shadow side. Each time

Baby screamed, threw books at me, or tore something off the wall, it was because he'd forgotten he wasn't supposed to do that. Again I'd beg him to stop doing this kind of thing and again he'd assure me that he would, that this had been the last time, such was our cycle and it bordered on insanity, but it also meant that I could relate to his forgetfulness, because with each new cycle I'd forget just how many times he'd already made this promise. This business of forgetting was necessary because my fear of abandonment was as strong the first day we met as it was the day he left me, and the fear that he'd leave me was one reason I tore open his wound, whenever I caught sight of it, which in turn led to Baby wanting to destroy me, which in turn gave me the moral high ground, which ended with Baby begging me not to leave him, instead of the other way around. Therefore, our conflict was not only logical, but also harmonious. So when he didn't actually hit me it tracked with the logic of our relationship, but however inevitable the violence was and however well I could explain why it was necessary, I didn't tell Elahe. Being able to say: 'He beats me,' or, as with my first boyfriend: 'He's raping me,' was a pedestal built for those without fault. For those who never asked for it. The statement ('He hurts me') was the finest of distinctions, and I had never been that good, that faultless. That's why it wasn't worth explaining what was going on to an outsider. Our harmonious conflict made intimacy a matter of life and death. Baby hated himself for his fierce temper and, at the height of his rage, he'd turn his anger on himself, punching himself in the face so hard it left bruises. Then we'd cry together and put our arms around each other.

No one was going to hurt my baby. Not even Baby himself. Thinking about it now made me wet. I'd thought I was indispensable to him.

Kenneth always had lunch at the same spot, a Thai restaurant in Hornstull where no one had ever seen the man behind the counter leave his chair. It's the best Thai in town, was Kenneth's defence when anyone complained about the monotony, because routines and regular habits made him seem his age. For most people, eating lunch in this heat was unthinkable but Kenneth had carefully mapped out his days to keep himself from slipping. Deep inside the darkness, he ate his chicken laab without rice, to keep his figure. I put the big bouquet of roses next to his plate and took a seat without saying hello. Flowers beside someone who was not worthy. And yet I would end up leaving the roses there, with Kenneth, who never gave anyone roses, nor did he receive them. He looked up from his plate with a flash of confusion and anxiety, but where would he go? It was just the two of us here.

'I've come to murder you.'

Kenneth snorted. 'I've been so busy these past few days, Bibbs.'

We both knew this was the worst possible excuse as our lives were so embarrassingly similar. We were never busy and only took on tasks we'd assigned ourselves. Before we could say anything else, a woman walked in and said: 'Kenneth,' as if Kenneth were the very man she was looking for. Kenneth sat back, relieved.

Milli was a photographer who had first made a name for herself photographing nightlife, when such a profession still existed. Through her thin linen shirt, I glimpsed the outline of her breasts, which I had seen once when Pripps beer took a group of us out for a swim in the archipelago. Her breasts were no more than a centimetre of perfect nipple. Nowadays she wrote about art in various lifestyle magazines, and had established herself as a surprisingly ignorant critic after a very successful exhibition about her experience as a diabetic. The images had been shown in a small gallery that gave anyone who knew someone a show. We were the same age and had been acquaintances for twenty years, I disliked her because she'd adopted a lisp after turning thirty along with a way of wrinkling her nose. And because I suspected she and Baby had fucked.

'Bibbs! I didn't recognise you with that dark hair.' Milli's hair was straight and gleamed like stainless steel.

If you spend your days in the city, you risk running into all sorts of idiots. The usual suspects and the ones you've forgotten, and therefore don't have the sense to worry about. Milli lived with a famous musician who, last I saw him, told me that in all the years with his band (which had been world famous) he'd been faithful and had turned away hordes of young women who'd thrown themselves at him. Because of Milli, back home. Do you understand? he repeated as we stood farthest inside the bar at Brillo. His success had waned, and by the time he returned home a normal man, Milli, who had sent him thousands of pictures of her long nipples, had stopped desiring him. They hadn't slept together for years and seeing girls on the subway would make him hard. 'I've always got a bit of a chub on,' he'd said, swigging his beer, 'but these days I'm just a dirty old man who looks like someone who used to be famous.' I hugged Milli with one arm, ignoring her hair comment. Her skin was as tight as a drum.

'Sorry to hear about you and Baby,' and the end of one eyebrow bent towards her hairline, instead of following her brow bone.

'What about me and Baby?' I looked at Kenneth and my palms started sweating. He was trying to sink back into himself. Someone walked in, but left again and we all looked towards the exit, our attention, for a moment, snagged. A radio was playing, perhaps in the back of the kitchen where there was a man we'd never laid eyes on. Otherwise the summer was quiet, we could see as much through the big window. Summer is quieter in general, unlike winter, with snow blowing across snow. Or autumn, the moisture in the bright orange ground, or spring for that matter, when everything splits in two, and then those two into another two. Milli turned to me again, eager to take back what she'd said, but there was no taking it back.

'Oh, sorry I thought. I thought you guys had broken up.'

'Nope, we haven't broken up.'

Kenneth cleared his throat and coughed, as if something were stuck in there. Milli said: Kenneth what's going on. Kenneth said: I've started smoking again.

'Well, OK, we did break up, but it's fresh. How do you know?'

'Oh, Bibbs, sorry I. . .'

'Did Kenneth say something? Because I told you that in confidence,' and I gave Kenneth an accusatory look, but Kenneth didn't look guilty in the way you might if you've gossiped about a rape.

'Oh, Bibbs, sorry.'

Milli told me that she had seen Baby and Nina, the fat actress from Örkelljunga, canoodling the night before, while I'd been chasing happiness elsewhere. No, not even 'happiness'. 'Happiness' was too ambitious. I'd felt confident and went after a sum of money with my name on it, wondering if there was some out there that I didn't already know about. There was so much in the world, and so little set aside for me. While I'd been removing a man's belt, Nina and Baby had been canoodling in Blecktornskällaren, that living altar for drunks to die on. Day also emerges from day, as does night, even if I'm not there to see it. Blecktornskällaren, which served fried fish and frozen peas, some thawed, some not. An institution frequented by teenagers and lovers, the lovers because it simply doesn't matter where you go when you're in love and you have to prove it. Fat Nina. . . and there I was struggling to be thin for Baby, thinking he loved me in spite of my rolls of fat, not because of them. What I was learning about my man's preferences made his love feel less real. Baby hadn't sacrificed his true desires for me. He hadn't sacrificed anything, and I had sacrificed so much. Milli described them standing at the bar, hugging acquaintances, while Nina laughed out loud. Baby had enjoyed making her laugh. They had kissed and held each other and Milli had heard him say:

'I want the world to know.'

How could the world be so small to him, that it was only me, I thought, but Baby got what he wanted: I knew. Milli kept talking, but my anxiety howled. Kenneth's mouth was moving, as was Milli's, I nodded but the noise drowned out the voices, and the summer, so far silent, was now deafening. How long had Baby been planning for someone new? I knew it was hard to keep him faithful and the first year I put everything into preventing him from cheating by being the Bibbs implied by the name, the person his friends delighted in asking about. But it was exhausting to be the stereotype of a woman, and in the end it cost me less to keep him with my screaming, and through catastrophe bind him to me. Whichever path I chose, the job of being with Baby robbed me of my rest and that was why I had aged, even though not ageing was what this whole business was about. As long as he did what I wanted, it was worth my effort. Elahe once said that only a crazy woman would believe that man could be faithful, but this was why I, Bibbs, intended to succeed. Nina being in that kitchen was a sign that my hard work had been for nothing. I felt stupid for failing to prevent this love affair. My mission, I had mistakenly thought, had been to prevent the cock from—

'Nina? My friend Nina?'

'You're not exactly friends,' Kenneth said, and I said to Milli: *I* left *him*. I repeated, *I* left *him*. I was hot and I had the shivers. The roses on the table, not wrapped in paper. Because he'd have put them in water right away. Two shades of pink roses, one cerise and the other barely pink, like the suggestion of pink. There was meaning behind my choice and I would have excitedly explained it to Baby, to remind him of my ingenuity and brilliance. When I saw Baby with that other body in the window, I thought that I must have misunderstood something. My eyes had deceived me. There was just someone there for the time being. Maybe Baby was buying sex now, too. Or was having a one-night stand. But Nina, who won prizes and got interviewed by the morning news. Not just the evening news. Nina who, before she made it, used to write to say she loved me and had read my blog. You're brave, she wrote, and she had taken the courage I'd offered up for free all those years and put it in her heart and shot herself into space and become a fixture. Because she knew a few things I didn't, but I could have learnt those things had I wanted to. Had I wanted to. All the daily errands took time away from what could be developed into talent. Nina was, after all, a fan. My fan. Don't trust your fucking fans. Mickey had warned me, but I would promptly. . . Now this devastation, and this betrayal. Milli got up to order, as if she hadn't just put a bullet through my heart. I wanted

Baby to come pick me up and take me away. From these evil people. We'd got lost in the night, no more, and now we could go back home. Come. I thought: I have to call Baby and ask him. Because something had gone wrong. He wanted to have a child with me. I'd been a child with him. We went to couples therapy and alcohol therapy and therapy for his rage. We'd been in all kinds of therapy. I had put in the time and the consideration and God knows what. I was still looking forward to the returns. I'd given him all my money and then he had given me his. I took it, but never with the same relish. He hated paying for me, just like he hated giving me everything, even the little things, no matter how small. Yet he always demanded more. As if he were the day itself. Sometimes when he came home from work and asked: What have you done today? I'd say: Worked out. But had I? It was different from time to time. But my biggest reason for doing anything was to set the scene of myself for Baby. There was no difference between doing things and pretending to do them, as long as it ended with him saying 'Well done, darling' and stroking my hair.

How could he, I said, and the colour had returned to Kenneth's face and he was saying something about Nina's character, like, she wants to have you? No, she wants to be me, I replied.

There's no chance in hell, you know, that he'd have a shot with someone like her, if it wasn't for me. I'm his erotic capital. He gets to sleep with famous people because I'm famous.

Milli said, lost in reverie: 'Baby has always been handsome.'

I stood up.

It'll be over soon, Kenneth said. What, are they a couple? I said.

Kenneth and Milli were menacingly united in their silence.

I have to leave, I said, and I did leave. I've always thought Hornsgatan was the ugliest street in Stockholm and I hated walking it. As I walked past the ugliest building on the ugliest street, I called Kenneth. How long have you known, I asked as soon as he answered. Just a couple of weeks, Bibbs. Just two weeks. Three, four.

Sometimes when I crossed Västerbron I thought about the people who chose to throw themselves off the bridge and decided they were cry babies. On Hornsgatan it was impossible to throw yourself off because it's the kind of street you throw yourself down onto, from the wall of rock or the small windows of the apartments where we'd go to afterparties, ten years ago, fifteen. Sometimes the thought of time gone by was dizzying. In the mornings when we were young and at afterparties in those buildings, we'd ride the elevator down to take money out at the ATM, then ride up again to avoid meeting the dealer on the street. The biggest thing we had was that we had nothing, time lay before us like a riddle no one cared to articulate. Who could have guessed who would die, or how many would end up being sober alcoholics. We didn't understand how much money there had been and how poorly we were managing it. Editors paid for columnists in national newspapers to write piece after piece about a night-club in Stockholm and they printed whole spreads about the jeans a particular person thought you should buy. No one could have guessed how little would remain. I had no desire to die but wondered how I was going to manifest thirty-nine identical years. The finesse required for the life that lay behind me seemed to belong to youth. Finesse and ambition and inventiveness and a sense that beauty and recognition mattered. Fatigue hit me like a sledgehammer. Living is above all the ability to make decisions, and to stand up for the decision you have made, and for some time now I'd been plagued by enormous uncertainty. Or a constant ache, that everything was more complex than it had seemed, like a ray of light refracted through a crystal. How it reveals itself against the wall. Nowadays I lingered over the pictures I took, not to register every physical flaw, but because I thought they were ridiculous. I read the emails I got and they seemed irrelevant. When I'd sat with Nina at Tennstopet and she'd talked about daring to do this or that, I hadn't been jealous of her absolute belief that what she was offering the world was new. No, I was filled with a mature tenderness. She would have to find out for herself that everything had already been discovered. Who was I to rob her of that happiness.

Mickey called and I answered. Did you know? I asked, and he claimed he didn't. I explained what had happened and he didn't ask any follow-up questions, as if he knew. The buses jerked by on the street, like plump, horny seals. I'd lived through all this before, and moreover I'd lived through it more than once. I'd lived through all this twice over. Heartbreak, grief and conflagrations. Personal bankruptcy, cell changes, fights with neighbours. Mickey said: Bibbs. Baby feels no solidarity towards you. Why should you feel it towards him? Isn't it a continuation of the violence, you protecting him now? If you later regret it, after Nina takes their relationship public, and everyone will see that she's taken your man, then you'll never be able to speak out. About what he did. Because then! People will think you're motivated by revenge.

Mickey kept talking but the number 4 was passing by, so I had a hard time hearing him. The bus stopped at the intersection and people spilt out, gasping for air. I said, revenge isn't the issue here, Mickey. It's about right and wrong. The law is not vengeful, I said, and you're the law too, Mickey said.

Well, then I guess I have a responsibility to Nina, I said, yes, to all women, Mickey said.

One time we came across an abandoned house in the woods, Baby and I, while we were visiting his dad. He said to me, from atop a stone wall encircling the house, 'I want kids, Bibbs.' I believed everything he told me, except that. I believed in the good times, even when the times were at their worst. I believed in money magic. Money magic is spending money to attract more money. I believed the world could be divided into nerds and idiots. Baby and I were idiots, and Nina was a nerd. Kenneth and Elahe also nerds, Mickey idiot and Texas nerd. I believed in making unpopular decisions. But imagine believing in that, in being a woman with children. With Baby nonetheless, of all the idiots and nerds who walked this earth. I had laughed and walked into the abandoned house, and I had a heightened feeling, like someone was filming us.

As if we were performing this because we had to, as if the relationship were holding a gun to our heads and saying: 'Go on, say it.' Loving each other as Baby and Bibbs was a mirage in the desert, a desert that was about loving each other as man and woman. Man and woman kept us from revealing who we actually were, and in place of a floor in the abandoned house was grass and trampled earth. Tall white snapdragons were growing through other bushes. Someone had lit a fire and tagged the ruins. Leev, it said. Where would we live, I asked. Slipgatan is too small. Here, Baby said, and gestured at the ruins. We'll live here.

I wanted to be buried by Baby's side, but living by his side was more difficult. Hadn't I longed for a way out, even though I'd never been interested in suicide? I was interested in setting things in motion, not stopping them. Furthermore, suicide was a misguided attempt at changing the inevitable. OK, I had no regrets. OK. I was just wondering if everything I'd done was right. Baby would have said that this was the crisis. The crisis that makes me not work like I should be working. The crisis that makes me eat and then take my shirt off and stand in front of the mirror. What did my breasts look like before? Maybe he was right, this was the crisis, but it was also a loss of previously held ideals and an engulfing void behind me, because I didn't know which other ideals might also be available to me. I thought of every possible exit strategy. Start a clothing store. Move. Suicide was the only option I never considered. With the exception of this afternoon on Hornsgatan. To make sure those bastards would never be happy again.

I walked into a supermarket at Zinkensdamm, wishing I was in Vasastan. Vasastan is the only part of the city that feels like a city. At the corner of Frejgatan and Dalagatan you could buy a cup of coffee for fifteen. Baby thought the coffee should cost ten. In Zinken, the vending machine coffee cost ten. Below the vending machine sat a white curly-haired dog without a leash. I greeted the dog. The clerk looked like a drowned corpse. Is that your dog, I asked. Nope, he replied. The dog comes in and hangs out, that's all. I tried to get a look at the dog's face. A man appeared through a wall of milk cartons.

'The usual?' I looked over my shoulder but I was alone there.

'Excuse me.'

'So, the usual?'

The man looked at me as if he and I were acquaintances and I knew why I seemed familiar to him. However, I wasn't allowed to pretend to know why, because they hated that. They liked it better when I played along. I pretended to think.

'You must be mistaking me for someone else.'

I saw that it had dawned on him who I was. He became brash.

'Then why are you standing there like we know you.'

I excused myself, took the coffee, and left the store but remembered that I had forgotten to buy what I'd gone there for and went back inside.

'One pack of blue Camels and a lighter,' I said to the young guy. The shopkeeper was talking to the dog. The guy at the cash register was a summer temp. Everything he punched into the machine beeped in error.

'Any vacation to look forward to?' I asked.

The older man had moved behind the other conveyor belt, opened and shut the cash drawer.

'I guess there'll be two or three days in August.'

I nodded.

'That's more like a regular weekend,' I said.

The man said: I'm going to the storeroom. I picked up the cigarettes and the coffee cup with the same hand and left. Outside the door were buckets filled with the flower I associated the most with my childhood.

It was now perfectly clear that Kenneth didn't think my problem with Baby was worth a loan of 100K. He had told me, without telling me. Perhaps he had his doubts because Baby had managed to develop his personal brand with a younger woman while I was still getting older. I couldn't possibly tell Kenneth the truth, that I needed the tobacco shop near Slipgatan and that I had lost my way. It was too involved and not as spectacular. Baby had probably accused me of things too, so for Kenneth the question of who was to blame was tricky and difficult to relate to. For me, the blame was not difficult, neither to place nor to bear. Mathematically, it was a simple formula, because the blame can be repaid and made good. The shame was worse. There was no certainty that the shame could earn you credit. Baby was strictly controlled by shame and tried to fend it off by working with something he hated and not making more than a half-hearted attempt to change it, not enjoying sex and drinking himself into oblivion. When we were newly in love, he accompanied me to the afterparty at the Grammis music awards and got brain-fucked by the brown liquor. In the taxi on the way home, his head drooped to his chest and he let a loud one rip in the taxi, where otherwise the only sound was car wheels on asphalt, in the long tunnel leading to Hagaparken. He was too drunk to know what he had done, but the shame he usually bore was passed on to me. Such is shame. It poisons. The driver had been telling me about his dream of owning a vineyard and rephrased the last line of his story:

'It's between the ground and God,' but said 'him' instead of 'the ground'.

'It is between him and God.'

Baby was so drunk that night he wasn't there anymore, and for the first time my glorious mission as his girlfriend felt like hard work. When we got home, I dragged him through the door and onto the bed. Baby came to life as I was washing off my make-up; I heard him open the fridge to pour a glass of wine, which he downed in one gulp, before falling asleep. How much would Kenneth have lent me for that night and every other one like it? The anecdote was too embarrassing and I was loyal to Baby's image of himself because that image was connected to my own. Of course it was hard to do any other work while I was working for Baby, Kenneth should have understood as much. Even there, the question of who was indebted to whom was murky because in the beginning helping him home and counting the glasses without anyone noticing had amused me. Three, four, five was fine. More than seven, then my legs got jumpy and I started to sulk. Baby would ask what was wrong, even though he knew the answer, and I'd say it's nothing. Besides, Baby was good, perfect, in the daytime, and bad at night, whereas I was good at night, but worse during the day.

Looking down on the tower cranes at Slussen, they seemed to belong to the sky, and the spire of Riddarholmen Church rose from the horizon. Sometimes all you could think was: Stockholm, you beauty. A woman had paused beside me to drink from her water bottle. She drank in a hurry, water dribbling out the corners of her mouth; we only looked at each other for a second. I left my paper cup on a power box. The coffee hadn't cooled. One winter, I'd stood at the top of the Katarina Elevator thinking: 'Why am I still here?' But where else would I go? And who would help me get there? I looked over Slussen again, the asphalt torn from the ground against its will. I let the gravity of the moment wash over me. A few years ago, I had felt no kinship with people whose lives seemed to be the result of other people's bargain-basement ideas, but with this view of the chaotic construction site, train tracks running alongside train tracks, I knew that no matter how strong the wish, you're helpless in the face of how it was meant to be.

'Friends,' I wrote beneath the image I'd chosen, a picture of my manicured hand reaching into the white sky, 'you know I've always been honest about who I am. Whether it was offering advice on how to learn to love your body or arguing with idiots on TV. In recent years, I haven't shared as much about my life as I'd have liked. I guess I've grown up and have been trying to focus on the people near at hand. But there's another reason I've stopped sharing. Unfortunately someone I loved and have lived close to for the past few years has done something unforgivable to me. I still have a hard time calling it rape, but if recent conversations have taught us anything, it's that sexual assault is a spectrum. In any case, what happened has led to a life change for me. I'm writing this to you all in order to set myself free. At the moment I have nowhere to live but am staying with a friend, who is taking good care of me. Please don't feel sorry for me and please don't put the name of anyone you think is guilty in the comments. I just wanted to tell you that now, once again, I know that I am strong. And if there's anyone else out there who needs to hear it, I know you're strong too. XO! Bibbs'

I read the post twice before publishing it, moved that in the midst of crisis I had the presence of mind to reach out to other women in need of support. Moved that I signed off with my name. This was the Bibbs we all knew. Bibbs as she was at the outset. I swiped down on my screen and someone had already commented. The confession was a deposition for Kenneth. The confession was my key to Slipgatan and the knife that severed me from Baby, cutting through the place where our bodies had fused together. To free myself. My confession was a capitulation: OK, Nina. If you want him so badly, go ahead, take him.

After posting the picture, I was filled with a kind of anti-energetic energy and walked quickly away from Slussen, taking the route to Skeppsbron along the water. The Grand Hotel was small. I'd staggered around that lobby, drunk, but I didn't want to dwell on that so I kept going, towards Kungsträdgården. When I met Baby, I didn't have a bicycle or any plants at home, but he had a snake plant. 'It's not supposed to bloom,' he'd told me when I called him at work, excited to tell him that it was blooming.

Everyone I encountered was casually dressed. I was wearing the same clothes as the night before, my sandals were rubbing the side of my foot and my T-shirt no longer smelt of the ordinary man's aftershave. It was too hot to keep my jacket on. Would the ordinary man believe what I'd written about Baby? Baby often said that he wanted to die and when I asked him if he was serious he'd hiss an incomprehensible reply, and even though he was never on his phone, I knew that he knew about my post. I could feel it in my skeleton. Deep in the bone. If marrow is what's inside a bone, then that's where I knew that Baby knew. I shut off my phone, out of fear. But hadn't he betrayed me too? At NK, I bought some perfume for 2,500. The first time Baby and I visited the city centre together, we went to Cow Perfumery and I bought three expensive perfumes without having smelt a single one. Outside the store Baby had hugged me, and I felt his cock get hard against my groin. My indiscriminate spending turned him on.

With the perfume in NK's summer bag, I moved on to the make-up department. How does a person answer the question, 'Did you rape her?' Who would be the first to ask Baby? A brief but self-righteous storm of jealousy swept through me. Nina would cry and ask if it was true. There was no denying that question, like there was no denying the question, 'Are you lying?' Any answer that wasn't a confirmation sounded like a lie. Baby couldn't deny it, and besides, where would he deny it? My voice had reach, he had no platform. I was his platform. At the Tom Ford counter, I wondered if Baby would be angry, or would he understand that I was working with what I had under the circumstances? Or did he care so little about me that he wouldn't even be upset.

The department store was full of people. Come September, everyone would be back to their determined rushing to the subway or commuter train, I thought. Now they were wandering around this mall, helpless without the meaning conferred by labour. On the top floor, I refreshed myself with a cold glass of wine, before taking the escalator down and exiting through the Sergelgången arcade. At the

Plattan part of the square a man was setting up a table with strawberries, bilberries and children's shoes. I stopped a short distance away and lit a cigarette. On an A4 page, the seller had written STRAWBERRIES, but nothing about the bilberries or the shoes.

'Where are the berries from?' I asked, stubbing my cigarette out.

'Sweden.'

We looked at each other, both aware of the lie, and I felt an intense affinity. I walked up the stairs where people had placed flowers for the dead after the terrorist attack. Restaurants with dishonourable reputations proliferated on and around Drottninggatan, flourishing restaurants and restaurants that had lost their liquor licence and were struggling. There were at least five jobs in each restaurant. I could have worked in a restaurant, but I lacked the requisite talent: the ability to prioritise. Up at Cityterminalen, three bricklayers were sitting on the ground and having a smoke. Bricklayers, I thought, such an old-fashioned occupation. The harder you work, the more visible your profession, that's how I knew I could get down to a size 40 the summer I met Baby.

Men whizzed past me on electric scooters, their faces blurred by speed. I walked into T-Centralen, where I took the green line to Odenplan.

In a month the bright colours would fade, exhausted by the persistent sun. The biggest change that came with age was that the things I desired were getting more expensive. A well-tailored coat gave away a woman's age, otherwise it was almost impossible to guess. Elahe said she knew she was getting older because young people in shops were no longer bothered about her, but since everyone recognised me, I hadn't noticed the difference between one kind of bother and another. Elahe also said that she knew she was getting older because things that had seemed important before weren't important anymore, and this was a poorly veiled criticism of my life. The man I went home with from the casino had guessed that I was thirty-nine and tomorrow I would be turning thirty-nine. Not too bad. Some people, by this age, had already been dead a long time. One noticeable difference, apart from my expensive taste, was that the indentations from my pillow lingered on my face in the mornings. My jaw-line had lost its sharpest contour a few years ago, my eyelids seemed heavier, and sometimes I caught myself thoughtfully tugging at a deposit of fat under my chin. Another change, I spotted in a subway window, was that I looked like crap when I was hungover. All in all, a small price to pay for being alive. I wasn't like my mother or Baby, I didn't want to die. I wanted to live and buy beautiful things. My love of things put a cap on the anxiety; paradoxically the buying of things created more anxiety. This kept me busy. My phone felt heavier when it was turned off, so I turned it back on. Two unknown numbers had called.

Odenplan station reminded me of a swimming hall. When I was younger, I occupied myself with things without really knowing why, and I often tried to recreate that magic, but it was hard. We weren't as attractive then. No one was, of course. Being constantly good-looking came later, around 2013, when we started taking pictures every day. Before that, it wasn't necessary because you were only visible the moment someone caught sight of you, or when Milli took a photo at Spy Bar with a slow shutter speed that only made its radiance visible after the fact. Everything was easier to get back then because there were so many things and so few people.

As I walked past Tennstopet, I tried to keep my eyes on the road, afraid of seeing Nina and Baby at one of the tables. Nina would never dare be together with a rapist, I knew that. As for me, it was a foregone conclusion that if Baby was accused of anything, I would stand by him. If my man is a thief, then I'm in love with a thief, I told myself when I wanted to forgive him. These eyes that seemed set on suffering were drawn to the patio as if to the scene of an accident. No one recognised me or knew what I had said about

Baby. Maybe nothing would change, not even Elahe with her morals wanted to know what men had or had not done. 'I can't believe it, actually,' she had said repeatedly when I told her that a mutual acquaintance had jerked off on his lover's thigh while listing her ugly qualities. Why wasn't it believable? But distrust also alleviated the proportions of my lie. No one would believe me and what does a lie matter if no one is listening. Kenneth wouldn't believe me either. But he was going to have to pretend.

I scrolled through my phone while waiting for the cars to stop at the intersection. Over a hundred people had already commented, and my pleasure contained a kernel of disgust. They finally got me, splayed open. The cunt turned inside out. Everyone could walk right up and stick their filthy fingers in. Nothing was as satisfying to people as a defeated woman and from now on they would think of my naked body getting pounded each time they saw me. And they'd say ugh, but when they pulled down their panties in the bathroom there'd be a wet spot. I didn't want to spend another second in front of Tennstopet. Nina had hung back on that patio in order to tell me that she'd taken my man. Not because she admired me, or wanted to collaborate. My arrogant way of speaking to her struck my head like lightning. How do you deal with the shame that surfaces when you realise you didn't take the hint after a child star told you about her labial herpes outbreak. I pictured the sores. My Baby. Nausea in my throat, what if I'd misjudged her! What if she thought, as I did, that violence was linked to intimacy and those two things made women of us. I was in the vice-grip of doubt. What if the violence wouldn't drive them apart, but rather would make them reach into each other's mouths, with devotion. I saw, like, two mouths meeting in close-up, tongues about to swallow each other and become one. I crossed at the crossing, convinced that mouths are the centre of the world's collective evil. The mouth that kisses you and makes you lose your senses, the mouth that lies and makes you believe that what the mouth is saying is true. How could he allow his tongue to stray. Yes, the truth shook me, but I told myself: 'Pull yourself together, Bibbs.' Many, but not me, thought ignorance was preferable. True love demands EVERYTHING. Even the ingrained shit and burning fire. My lie, in comparison to Baby's, just seemed like a sloppily told anecdote. No one could be convicted of rape and people never managed to remember what men had done. Half the editorial staff at DN had beaten their wives and Kenneth once had sex with a sleeping teenager and I'd said that Baby had done the same to me, even though it wasn't true. Culturally, my crime – wrongfully accusing someone of rape – was more severe, I knew it was; at the same time *someone* should absorb the unsolicited blows that had come my way. The night-time slaps from my first boyfriend, or the friend who'd held my head down on his cock until I vomited on his stomach. And afterwards I was the one to apologise, because vomit was gross, and my friend accepted the apology as if it had been his to take. Who would make that up to me? Unfortunately, it fell to Baby. If he thought I wasn't going to take anything away from him. If he'd been hoping I'd leave Slipgatan and never return. He was wrong.

I can burn everything-everything down. It's not even mine.
Given the choice, I wouldn't have bought it in the first place.

Anxiety loosened its grip on me as I decided to cut through
Vasaparken. Marite used to say that nature instilled harmony.
Families sat on the grass like impenetrable engine rooms,
peering in was futile. Nothing displayed on the blankets
revealed anything about how the inner machinery functioned.
Someone shouted my name and I raised my hand, a reflex.
I was a machine you could stick a coin in and get a greeting
from in return. People who got their kicks shouting at people
they didn't know were bums and their attention meant that
they'd never be happy but I would still try. Me being fat,
that's not good enough, I have to be really fat. If I tell a funny
story, I'm supposed to follow up with another one right
away. If I post a picture, they need to know where I bought
the sweater, so they can have an opinion about the sweater's
price, is it cheap or expensive. I am at their mercy. No, I mean
service. On the other side of Vasaparken, I waited at another
crossing. At this time of year, you shouldn't be keeping an eye
out for the airport bus, you should be looking out at the sea
and noticing three different shades of blue. Sky blue, sea blue,
and the blue that arises where the two meet. I crossed Sankt
Eriksbron. On one side of the bridge were beauty salons and
on the other side fitness shops. I wondered how they were
managing. It was one of the many things I asked people that
annoyed Baby. How are you managing? But many of our
acquaintances were thin with a corpulent energy. When we
walked around Djurgården on Sundays, we'd bump into my

old friends who'd become TV personalities, comedians, and producers. People who boasted about how little they were doing a decade ago were now talking about how much they were doing. I have a clear memory of what their faces used to look like, puppyish and open, they'd just moved here from some backwater place, holding out their dream for all to see. Back then they were all employed by the same two television channels run by the same three men who enjoyed being jerked off full-time, and my acquaintances worked as their jerk-offs. As if a clenched fist weren't a weapon, but a hole to stick your dick in.

I forgive them, I thought, magnanimously. I get it. There is no such thing as easy money. There's no such thing as a 'free lunch' and a legitimate criticism of these old friends who hung out in Djurgården was that they refused to acknowledge what this had cost them. I'm an old player in the game. I was born here. I didn't roll in from the countryside one day, bright-eyed and bushy-tailed, so I have it in me to acknowledge that the most sacred things go for a much lower price than one imagines. The truth is, the moment you enter into negotiations you've lost. Mickey and I always knew we didn't work with glamour. We worked as travelling salesmen and we lowered our price when we had to lower our price. 'Bibb's voice' and the contrived proximity were worthless, it turned out. Only a few things cost everything-everything. My pride, unfortunately, was practically free and if there was redress to be had, this was the day I'd find out what that cost. My redress was Slipgatan. Maybe Slipgatan had cost me my youth, the knife, and then they got Baby at no extra charge. I almost wished, as I approached Fridhemsplan, that it had cost less, but I wasn't the one who decided the value of one thing or another. How do you explain who sets the price? It's like an invisible hand descending and rearranging everything, if you can imagine that. An invisible hand with no emotional ties to the people it tugs at. The stretch between Sveavägen and Fridhemsplan was the only part of Stockholm that reminded me of elsewhere and if I remember correctly I didn't run into anyone. Soon it was evening and night would follow, it too stifling and flat. Everyone was going around waiting for rain, a state to which Stockholmers were unaccustomed and it gave the city a certain European air. It was making us all cocky.

I don't want to say I was already having regrets by Wednesday morning, but I was concerned that my disclosure hadn't exactly led to resolution. What I was imagining felt like something being pieced together after the fact. Yes, the money, but mostly I'd wanted Baby to suffer. It was impulsive, I admitted to myself, hugging Elahe's long pillow. An impulse resembled a lie in one troubling respect: it couldn't be retracted. I put another pillow between my thighs to relieve my aching hips. During the night, I had woken up a few times and checked the app, without offering up a sign of life, either to my followers or to people I knew. After reading the post again, I was still pleased with how I'd expressed myself. Elahe's room was boiling hot and it had been hard to sleep because I hadn't pulled down the blind. By the time I got out of bed, Baby had called twelve times, and Marite had called, and Elahe and a number I didn't recognise. Kenneth, on the other hand, had neither written nor called. I checked my account. No money.

In the living room, I turned on the projector and arranged my food on the coffee table. The night before I'd bought sourdough bread and fennel salami, tomatoes on the vine, and freshly squeezed juice. My birthday breakfast. I checked my phone. Only a few accounts had written anything nasty, or critical, and I perceived in unison the concern and the anger directed at Baby. Several girls had DMed me long rape stories and I wondered why. Their lack of boundaries repulsed me. Nothing was sacred. Marite had written that she'd sensed this but hadn't wanted to warn me, because I was already pathologically preoccupied with bad signs. I was eager for Elahe to come home. Apart from Baby, she was the only one who tidied up after me and there were no clean coffee cups left. The cups were stacked on top of each other and the few pieces of cutlery I'd used were scattered around the apartment.

Like Baby, Elahe was confident in her daily chores and she did them in succession, without thinking twice. No, this wasn't my home and my mess didn't suit the apartment. Slipgatan, on the other hand, with its yellow light. The knife twisted. Had Baby eaten Nina's ass in our bed.

I plugged the HDMI cable into the computer and got PornHub up on the screen. As I was putting on a relatively long stepson video and making my first sandwich, the phone started ringing. It was Mickey, who couldn't get a handle on his circadian rhythm.

'Damn, Bibbs, that was powerful. Yes, damn powerful. Take a look at this.'

He held his arm up to the lens to show me that his hair was standing on end. It was dark around him and his face looked hunted in the small pool of light.

'Yo, that was a crazy thing for me to do. I can't believe I did that.'

'Oh, but I can! You've always stood firm in your truth, Elisabeth. Yes, I'm fucking calling you Elisabeth now, the name your mother gave you. She should be proud!'

The porno was noisy and I turned the volume down.

'I don't know, Mickey, plenty of people have already done something like this,' I said with humility.

'You're so fucking on point, and you have a way of actually sounding honest.'

'Mickey, I AM being honest. Don't fucking start doubting me now.'

'No, no, that's not what I mean. I'm just saying, you have a quality that makes people believe what you're saying! You really have never been afraid of anything, Bibbs.'

Mickey was wrong. I'd always been afraid. I'd sought a similar fear in others, but no luck. Yes, I was always afraid when I threw myself off, but I was also afraid when the day was calm. The fear made no difference but it went on gnawing, patiently, inside me. Mickey cheered on everything I said and did and comforted me when things went too far. When I wrote that a beloved politician looked like a fat cow, or when I argued with my ex-lovers on my blog, or when I got caught shoplifting at NK and spoke out about it in *Expressen*. As long as I made the damage visible to the consumer, he comforted me. The comfort and forgiveness acknowledged me as what I was: hopeless. And Mickey didn't love me because I had a knack for hiding my flaws. He loved me because I was the best at being the worst. Mickey's video image started lagging and I could see him talking, but couldn't hear anything. On my phone, I checked my bank account (nothing) as well as the app where activity was happening of its own accord. A feminist name-and-shame account had reposted my post and added to their carousel a picture of me and Baby from a movie premiere. Baby's face was pixelated. I went back to FaceTime.

Mickey's voice resurfaced and I asked what the next step was. The video lagged when he started moving around the room.

'The next step? Step towards what? You've got this banked now, or what do you mean?'

On the projection screen the young guy with his dick peeking out of his underwear seemed to be talking to someone behind the camera.

Marite had said that her job was easy, because everyone had a natural connection to the other side, and could, if they so wanted, learn to hear the dead. Perseverance was the only requirement. If you got good at this form of mystical eavesdropping, you didn't have to be psychic, because the dead knew more about the future than the living and they liked to talk. 'But not just anyone can do what you do, Bibbs,' Marite said. 'That takes a very special talent. You're a master of not getting hung up on other people's unfortunate opinions about you.' Marite's praise warmed my heart, even now. I wouldn't get hung up on Baby's opinions about this. Mickey's voice was coming in choppy and I said,

'I can't hear you properly.' The stepmother walked into frame. She looked about my age.

In one day, I had gained 700 followers, but I didn't want them. I'd learnt to accept the followers I had from before, and I liked them in the sense that they helped me support myself. Before I moved to Slipgatan, much of my thinking time had been spent on figuring out how to keep them. Mickey had only just caught wind of YouTube and was encouraging me to start vlogging, but I didn't feel motivated to learn anything new. What I had once performed for my followers I was now performing for Baby instead, which until a few days ago had been at least as lucrative. On the phone, Mickey looked like face soup. Neither of us was made for the moving image. I hung up on him and turned up the volume on the video. The building across the street was so far away that the neighbours couldn't see what I was watching, and I longed for Slipgatan, where I used to watch videos of staged rapes in the living room, turned on by the fact that the neighbours could see, too. On Slipgatan the buildings were so close together it must have happened at least once, and this was an innocent form of thrill-seeking that Baby indulged because I had given up so much else.

While I'd been talking to Mickey, Elahe had written to me. She wasn't angry that I hadn't told her. She wasn't surprised either, although she was sorry that I'd had to suffer Baby for so long. This really wasn't worse than anything else he had done, she wrote. Elahe was overly critical of Baby and I started to type that she should calm down, but I put the phone down. Elahe and her husband were talking shit about us on their holiday, I'd heard, probably because Baby and I bickered about all sorts of shit. But we bickered because we thought all these sorts of shit were value-laden things that touched on 'Who the fuck are you in the depths of your fucking soul' and 'Who the fuck am I in the depths of my fucking soul' and could these two meet in a genuine encounter? Porn, I explained to Baby, was like eating when you were full or buying things you didn't need. It was a desire and my desires were never hidden from anyone, they were out in the open for all to see. Including the neighbours. Without their presence, the boy masturbating and the bud of the mother's butthole seemed dreary. Mickey's cluelessness in the face of my question about how to take this lie further had startled me. I didn't have a guilty conscience, but something was out of whack.

I made another sandwich and went back to the app. In the comments on my post, someone had tagged Baby's private account, which only had about a hundred followers. I deleted the comment and switched off the screen. As I bit into the bread, I tasted a large flake of salt, which rounded out the sweetness of the tomato, and in addition to this luxurious breakfast, I'd bought myself flowers, peonies. It would be almost a full year until it was tulip season again and you could hear the squeak of their long leaves rubbing together. Baby's story of how we met was embarrassing but I pretended it was charming, because if there was one thing Baby hated, it was criticism. One night when I was playing records in the wilds of Östermalm he'd come along to chat me up. When he told the story to my friends, I smiled but felt ashamed for him. The story didn't make him sound special. It made him sound like anybody. Sometimes I'd say to Baby, to help him be more special, 'I'd been waiting for you for years,' and in a way it was true. Baby was a weight around my ankles, grounding me. The herpes, for example. Before Baby, I'd never had an STD and Baby gave me herpes. He never admitted to infecting me, but comforted me with how common it was, and that he had it too. Sure, everybody had herpes, but I hadn't caught it yet. I'm sure you were already carrying the virus before you met me, he said when I got my first outbreak and there were so many sores I whimpered each time I peed. The sores ran like a constellation along the nerves of my groin from the skin over my clitoris down to my anus. At first his explanation sounded implausible, but after a while, on Slipgatan, I started to believe him. On Slipgatan, the truth was always up for discussion. Are you drinking again? I might ask when I could see that he was holding a beer during one of his sober spells, and he would deny it. 'No,' and meet my shifting gaze with his shiftiness. One night when Elahe and her husband were over for dinner, she heard our exchange and as we went down for a smoke on the street, she told me to stop asking questions that I already knew the answer to. 'You can see that he's drinking,' she said, 'so just tell him to stop.' I couldn't do that. Because on Slipgatan, reality was distorted, or at best doubled. The sobs caught in my throat and I held them there when he decided to come off the wagon or when I could tell, from the back of my thighs, that another outbreak was on its way. You're blowing it out of proportion, Baby would say about everything that mattered to me. But the sores were more evidence in the trial of my ineptitude. My pussy, which had been the last beautiful thing on a body that had so little youth left in it, was now ugly too, and could make others ugly. Sometimes I thought of Baby giving me herpes as a romantic gesture, and if it wasn't love he felt for me, then at least he felt sorry for me. Since I had a hard time separating the two feelings, I assumed he did, too.

A message popped up on my computer from Milli, who hadn't written to me in years.

'How are you Bibbs? I had no idea.'

'We're all clueless about what we don't know,' I replied. Milli was the first person I responded to, and I thought of Mickey, who hadn't had any good suggestions. No one works harder for you than you.

Milli was friends with a media woman called Bodil and Bodil really wanted to have me on her podcast, Milli texted. I don't know, I texted back. I don't know if I'm ready to talk about this yet. It's a safe space, Milli assured me, and people would be writing about me anyway. I was playing hard to get because I'd been waiting a long time to be invited on Bodil's podcast. In fact every woman in Stockholm had already been a guest, plus a few from Gothenburg, but not me. Bodil used to stay late at afterparties and let the gays snort coke off her breasts, and had been the editor of a book about choosing to be child-free. Then she became a mother, and at an afterparty shortly after giving birth, one of the more famous gays asked if she'd let him nurse, and she did. Milli took one of her last party photos that night, and the photograph had never been shown to anyone but there were ten or twelve of us who knew it existed. It was the end of a world in which you could smoke inside and I was sitting at the long end of a kitchen table, my head tipped back against the wall. Cigarette ash fell on my lap, I flicked it off my trousers, and it left a grey stain. I didn't say much, as was often the case if you finally met me, and when Bodil whipped her big breast out of her vest and everyone started screaming and laughing, I thought that of the two of us, I'd be the one to come out on top. The thought had been so convincing that I mistook it for the truth. The man who had impregnated her owned several properties and when I ran into her a few years later in Birkastan, she had just started a production company. I sent a few sardonic words to Mickey about her project, but my thought, about which of us would win, wavered. The next time I saw her, she had bobbed her hair. Every woman over the age of thirty-five was bobbing her hair and standing sassily with her hands on her hips. By then her podcast had become one of the most influential in Stockholm and she had thousands of female listeners.

'If you're on Gotland this summer, you must stop by,' she said. I kept smoking and she put her hand over her nose.

'Excuse me,' she said. 'I just can't stand the smell.'

Being invited on Bodil's podcast to talk about myself as an ordinary woman with ordinary experiences seemed like an opportunity: her 200,000 listeners might be able to answer the question of whether or not my disclosure had been worth anything.

'Please think about it,' Milli wrote when I pretended to hesitate. 'It would be a kindness to all women.'

I will remember that Wednesday forever. I'd placed the peonies on the dining table, after carefully cutting a few inches off the stems. The boy on the screen was close to climax, but I wasn't wet. 'You know what's nice about Mickey?' Baby had said to me once when we were on our way home after a dinner with Mickey and Texas. 'His weight yo-yos,' and I felt so loved as a fellow yo-yoer that I squeezed his hand tightly until he started laughing.

'Let go, that hurts.' Baby would find out that it hurt more when I let go than when I held on. A frightened thought I used to repeat for myself was: 'Imagine that everyone you know is dead,' and then I'd think: 'This will be true for one of us,' and then Baby would seem incredibly far away even though he was only at work. Mickey wasn't going to call, I realised. Noncommittally, I tried to masturbate, but couldn't find a rhythm. Even if the neighbours had been closer, it would have been hard to make out what was on the screen in the daylight and I got up to open the door a crack, as if it had opened by accident. Then I turned up the volume and went back to masturbating. I tried to fantasise about someone hearing me, but still no vibe. I cupped my hand over my pubic bone. Imagine that everyone you know is dead. This will be true for one of us. Then this won't matter at all.

People have stupid ideas about how to maintain a lie, but there's only one way and that's to let the lie move through the blood. Let the lie mix with saliva and seep out of your wounds, and become breath, so when the lie comes out of your mouth, voice loud, it sounds true. Even to the body from which it comes. Around lunchtime on Wednesday I went to Bodil's home after blow-drying my hair and Milli promised to come, too. I was wearing a bra and I don't know what I was hoping for, but I was hopeful. Bodil had ordered food and apologised for not cooking. But it all happened so fast, she said, unpacking the containers of food. 'Necessity knows no law.' At Bodil's, necessity was cod loin with melted butter, mashed potatoes, fresh shrimp, and sweet green peas. The whole apartment was painted in pastels, and the hues played off each other from room to room. The hall was pale pink, the living room pale green and the dining room a pale, pale yellow. 'I guess I *am* a little nuts,' she said, about the colours. Milli came into the dining room, did you order dessert? she asked, not saying hello.

Of course I did! Bodil said, clasping her hands in a way that make her rings clack. 'Desperate times call for desperate measures!'

Bodil had lost all her baby weight and was thinner than when she was young. She placed a cool hand on my shoulder and her lilac silk midi skirt made her blonde bob look silvery.

'Is it real?' I asked, standing in front of a Jenny Holzer.

Bodil smiled.

'Sten gave it to me when my company celebrated its fifth anniversary.'

Milli, Bodil said, will you get the wine. Milli came back with a bottle of white, cut the foil and pulled out the cork. She poured the cold wine into delicate glasses and the minerals bubbled and the glass fogged.

I had taken off my slides and was the only one of the three of us who was barefoot.

'Cheers,' Milli said, and we raised our glasses, before pulling out the chairs and taking our seats. The wine was dry and crisp with no bite, even though it was the first thing I had eaten or drunk all day. The acid lingered on the back of my tongue.

'Well, getting straight to the painful part. . .' Bodil said.

I explained that I didn't know what to say.

'Of course, no stress. You don't have to share any details, of course.'

Milli shook her head. 'I never liked him.'

'Yeah no, for sure,' Bodil said. 'There's always been something a little off about him.'

'But this off. . . I had no idea,' said Milli.

'No of course, not this off.'

I had already emptied my glass and Bodil reached for the bottle and refilled it.

'Excuse me for reaching. Back when he was working at Acne, people still thought he'd make something of himself. As we did about every hot shop assistant! But that's years ago now.' Milli pointed to her glass, and Bodil refilled it. 'Sten and I were talking about it this morning, and Sten was devastated. Sten is a feminist, after all.' Milli hummed. 'And he knows the HR director at the H&M group.' Milli gasped. 'We can make sure that this is his last day, Bibbs. If that's what you want.'

What did I want. What was hiding in that hope. An expectation dressed up as a promise.

The fish was flaky and melted like butter in my mouth, and the actual butter on top tasted crisp. The mashed potatoes were made with cream.

My fish is lukewarm, I said.

Bodil touched her heavy carved-gold earring. Do you want me to heat it up?

No, it's delicious, thank you.

The front door slammed again. Sten is home, Bodil said.

Hi Bibbs, Sten said after giving Bodil a kiss.

Hi Sten, I said.

I remembered Sten in the nude, bending over to pick up his jeans. His buttocks parted and I looked into the gulf of his ass. The gulf was like Sten's way of being, empty.

It's been a while, he said.

Yeah, all good, I said. Sten was tanned from all the tennis he played outdoors and his arms were sinewy, but the skin below his biceps looked loose, like Kenneth's. Nonetheless, he had it in him to wear a T-shirt. Around his right wrist was a large watch, complementing his good taste with a nod towards ostentation. That watch had been on my bedside table many times and he had told me about when he bought it, but it was a dull story. Sten used to kneel in front of me and suck on my breasts. One night when he was very coked up, he was sucking my breast and looked up at me sweetly. 'Mummy,' he said, but in French. 'Maman.' I stood up. What the fuck are you saying? It was an involuntary impulse, a chemical reaction like when two substances meet and before you know it, everything's gone up in smoke. When I realised what I'd done, I tried to smooth it over and urged him to continue. Under no circumstances should men feel criticised if you want them to put up with you. 'Come back, my boy,' I coaxed, but it was too late. It was the last night we shared, and the following year he proposed to Bodil with a ring made of white gold and set with fair-trade diamonds.

Maybe he was thinking about this too when he saw me, but nothing in his face suggested as much. In fact, he looked at me as if we were meeting for the first time. No one was talking anymore, and silence took hold of the room, which had been uneasy. Everything opened up in me but instead of tumbling out, as it usually did, it floated. I thought about a dream I'd had for a long time, of a different life, and for the first time in ages I wasn't seeing all the opportunities that had passed me by; instead I saw all the opportunities that were still to come my way. Sten had almost been my husband, and this apartment had almost been mine, and the cool hand on my shoulder could have been my own hand, on someone else's shoulder. The change was only a hair's breadth away, as was Jenny Holzer, being skinny, and buying sandstone for the farm on Gotland and having dinner with the playwright next door. Marite always said. . . What was it that she said. Change comes at a price, yes, but hadn't I paid? Hadn't I paid for another chance, when I threw Baby into the cold water off Västerbron? Bodil's invitation meant she thought we shared something. She recognised that what was beaten in me was also beaten in her. Community was never built on force or will, how could I have ever thought so? Community was based on acknowledging one's suppression, and boy did I acknowledge mine. If confession was the price, I confessed. If you say my life is a crime, I'm willing to atone.

'We're sitting here talking about how much we hate men,' Bodil said, and Sten kissed her again.

'All right, girls, I'll let you get back to it.'

Bodil kissed him on the hand. I excused myself and took my phone into the bathroom with me.

Kenneth answered on the first ring. The tiles made my voice sound shrill.

Where are you? Kenneth asked.

At Bodil's house for lunch.

Which Bodil?

You know which one.

He did know which one and would have died for an invitation to Gotland, even if it were as dishonest as the one I got in Birkastan. They'd been good friends, all of them, before Kenneth lost his job, and his reputation. If Kenneth had received a fake invitation, he'd have pretended not to have understood the fake part. He'd have gone to Gotland over the Easter break and checked into a hotel, just so he could get in touch with Bodil or Sten and ask if he could stop by. They'd have had to say yes, even as they were wondering how the hell this had happened as they waited for his car to appear on the gravel drive.

I'm going to be a guest on her podcast, I said.

I'll transfer the money now, he said.

I sat down on the toilet. Every kilo in my body weighed double. Each bone and piece of cartilage between my bones was heavy metal.

Thank you, Kenneth, I said, and I meant it.

Say hello to Bodil, Kenneth said.

OK, I said. I promise.

In the dining room they were speaking softly, and I walked back in.

'There she is,' Bodil said. 'We're imagining an interview.

Where did you go,

is the opening question. Like, what happened to you,

and then you can talk about what you've been working on in recent years and well. You did that thing for

Maria Bingo,

you can talk about that. Then you can talk about your journey into
 body acceptance.
 That's been a major part of your
 presence. Brave.
 We need to talk about your "drugginess" of course,
 only in brief because I think it's good to mention it so it doesn't seem like we're HIDING anything.
 All of this is supposed to be like,
 girl talk. Like now, this lunch. That's the vibe.
 When you steal away from your kids for an hour and just, you know,
 meet up with your girlfriends and have two glasses of wine,
 in the middle of the day.'

I refilled my glass myself and said, I know, but I didn't know, and I'd never wondered.

'Then we'll talk about Baby and your
 yes your
 your
 and the power of admitting well yes I am in fact a victim.
 I am in fact.
 Why did he get to do that, and the comfort in being one of so many, so very many women who—'

'One of many what? What, one of many who have slept with Baby? Who else has?'

'Uh no, one of many women, who has been been been—'
Bodil was trying to find a word that wasn't rape, but still as
serious.

'Who are victims,' Milli said.

The line of women Bodil wanted me to join was longer
than history. It was hard to be at the back of the line, because
it looked more like a queue than a parade. I hadn't thought
about the consequences, what it would mean to stand behind
thousands who were saying 'Pick me, pick me' while they
cried and bled, muscles atrophied, loved because what other
choice did a person have. My stomach churned.

'No, but my thing isn't like that. I'm not. I haven't been.'

Bodil put her hands in her lap.

What do you mean Bibbs?

'I don't want to say that I'm one of them, or of you?
Or —'

It's easier to take back a big lie than a small one.

'What do you mean?'

I'd eaten a whole brioche without thinking and the carbs
were already in my body, determinedly heading to where
they would stick. I helped myself to more bread. It was all
too late.

'I don't want to call it rape,' I said, but I couldn't say more.
The bread in my mouth was so soft and the butter on the fish
was salty and sweet.

Bodil tilted her head.

'Of course we don't have to call it rape.'

Milli said: 'I'm sure you're not the only one who has experienced this with Baby,' and the thought of Baby's life

before Bibbs was searing. I wanted to change the subject but froze at the sight of Milli's mouth moving and out came the evidence that Baby had not been conjured by my love for him.

'I hope you don't mind but,' I heard a distant ringing, 'when we slept together.'

'And that was a hundred years ago,' Bodil assured me.

'Yes God another time, long before you two met,' Sten walked into the room, turned back around, 'it was only once but I felt that something was off.'

I could see Baby pushing himself into Milli, the whites of her eyes shining. In one of the pornos I liked to watch, one man entered a woman while another dragged her eyelids open with his fingers, making her look like a frightened animal.

Oh Baby, she said in my imagination. Milli, he said, Milli I love you more than Bibbs.

'What do you mean, off?'

'I mean, off. Just off. He's really not for me. That world is not for me.'

I drained my glass, but it was already empty and I searched for the right thing to say but instead I said, 'Which world?'

Milli was an anxious woman and often tugged at her fingers, which is why I never wanted to have a conversation with her that went beyond a friendly greeting, and if she happened to say something that caught your attention, she immediately wanted to take it back. She repeated:

'World, well no world in particular,' and tugged until her joints cracked.

Bodil interrupted, 'It was a different time, Bibbs. You can draw strength from each other.'

I took a fistful of mashed potato and smashed it against her closed mouth. The mouth that had been on Baby's mouth. With that sensual, natural curve of her upper lip. No, the mashed potatoes were finished. I said nothing. Bodil refilled my glass. Milli smiled, then Bodil, and then finally me. Excuse me, Milli said, and when she came back she had brought the glass pots of crème brûlée.

Is it OK if we skip the caramelisation, Milli said.

STEN, Bodil shouted, STEEEN, and Sten came into the dining room and took the pots to the kitchen. I remembered his buttocks exactly, because he was so thin it looked like his asshole was part of his back. We were all desperate for a new topic of conversation.

'Neither Milli nor I cook, do you?' Bodil said.

'No,' I said, refilling my glass, 'I prefer to eat.'

Bodil laughed a laugh that was meant to open up the room.

'I see that.' She repeated, 'I see that.' Then she said: 'I have the same problem.'

The ringing in my head that had been distant was now so overwhelming that I was having a hard time responding. What could she see? Milli said: Oh God, same here. A beeping started inside my head. Did Milli see it too? Milli said, we gorge ourselves on shrimp, don't we, Bodil?

Mm. Bodil said. And oysters. I excused myself and went to the bathroom and rinsed my face with water that was so cold it ached. The ache spread to my teeth, into my jaw.

Get back out there and do not eat another bite in front of those people, I said to myself.

I called Kenneth. Why are you calling again? I transferred the money. Are you drunk. You sound drunk.

I went back in. They were speaking more loudly. It sounded like they didn't know I was there. Sten had put the dessert on the table, the silky surface of the pudding had developed a crust.

'Would you like some dessert wine?' Bodil asked.

Bibbs, say no.

'Yes, please.'

STEEEN, the dessert wine. All right, dig in.

I didn't touch the teaspoon and neither did Milli nor Bodil. They looked at me and their eyes were empty saucepans. All right, dig in, Bodil urged. I leant back in my chair and noted her haphazard arrangement of flowers on the windowsill. The haphazardness was fake. Do you gamble, I asked, at the casino. Go on, it's time for dessert, Bibbs. Are you good at making Sten happy? I asked. Bodil's saucepans rattled. Sten brought out the dessert wine and poured it.

There you go, I'm your butler, he said. Milli smiled as if she were the one in receipt of everything Bodil was getting. A man can only submit to a woman when he wants to. A woman, on the other hand, does so against her will.

Cheers, we raised our glasses and their faces revealed nothing. Except that I was the one who should have come out on top in this life. In my early years as a celebrity, I made sure to greet shop assistants and turn the barcode towards me on the conveyor belt. Everyone was a spy, out to get me. Everyone was a spy, gathering information about how unpleasant I was and what I really looked like, that girl from MTV. And now a hundred years later, Bodil had seen me eating. Ten years ago, I was so nice to the store manager at Diesel that he invited me to his kid's birthday party and I went. Standing like the village idiot alone in the garden, all eyes on me. Baby took care of a lot of the upkeep for Slipgatan, but I took care of the cut flowers, and I made it look like they were growing out of, in, the apartment. Not like Bodil's flowers, arranged for a memorial. I should have won, because I was in front of the camera. I wrote the blog. I talked about my pussy. I wrote that a challenge producer on TV4 used my panties to jerk off in. I spoke out on a morning show about a producer on Kanal 5 being a bastard and how little I was being paid. I threw myself off. All the while Bodil was in the background, listening in. The difference between her and me was simply that I had happened to say: 'What did you say,' when Sten called me Mummy, and Bodil had been smart enough to keep her mouth shut. Sten, I misspoke. I am the rightful winner. My investment was larger.

'Do you like the dessert wine, oh yes, apparently you do,' Bodil said.

Laughter.

My glass was empty, again. Bodil had raised her spoon over her dessert and I did the same, under the influence of the strong, sweet wine, and as she stuck her spoon through the crust I disappeared into my dessert and didn't look up until it was all gone. Bodil had put her spoon down beside the glass pot, the crust untouched.

'Aren't you going to have a taste!' I wiped my mouth with a linen napkin.

'No,' she said, putting her slim hand on her slim stomach, 'I'm full. So terribly full.'

If Everything Comes at a Cost

Being skinny comes at the cost of feeling full. Lifestyle comes at the cost of loyalty. Success comes at the cost of intimacy, work comes at the cost of integrity and Baby comes at the cost of Bibbs. Marite had grabbed my hand, its knuckles scraped after I punched the front door, and forced me to stay seated when really I wanted to get up. Look at me, she said. Listen. You don't have to get on your knees. You don't have to be a dog.

I understood each word on its own but couldn't access the whole. Sure, at times I had made clumsy attempts to bargain with my doggishness. Played with the idea of drawing a line, but each time the line was crossed I'd decide that it was better to be a dog than nothing at all. If Baby hadn't forced me to get down on all fours, the ugly part of Hornsgatan would have done, or my name would have, my name which I didn't think suited me. These thin, rich women were dogs too. Good dogs, they had learnt to stand on two legs. But that didn't make them dogs any less. It made them circus dogs. Everything comes at a cost. Even the sun shimmering in the trees and the forest stretching out behind, if it's beauty you want access to. But I was never one of them, heartless with blood on my hands. I was too fragile. Too used to the pain. That's why I didn't need beauty either. Just a little companionship, darling. That's why I'd say: 'You don't love me,' when I meant, 'I don't love you.' That's why I could handle being afraid when I heard him come through the door, annoyed, because I called fear by a different name.

If I could have seen anything beyond Slipgatan, a cursed apartment near a bridge that led across the water to a lottery prize so unlikely so as to be of no use. But I couldn't. There was the shit or there was being Bibbs, alone, again. I suppose I also knew that my love was sickly. So if not him, then who? Who else knew everything about destruction? I had torn my hand from Marite's grasp and knocked over my teacup, spilling brown water on the cards on the table. She didn't move a muscle. A dream catcher hung in the kitchen window and now the whole staging of our interaction looked childish. As if Marite did not in fact have contact with the other side. She didn't know anything about me. Not one of the hundred cards she'd laid had been accurate.

I rang the bell and Kenneth opened the door. He was wearing a white shirt and jeans.

'Bibbs? What are you doing here?' I wanted him to be on his guard, but he wasn't. Invite me in. I felt nauseous after the cab ride. It was nearing nine o'clock.

'Were you at Bodil and Sten's all this time?'

Aren't you going to invite me in? I said, and Kenneth stepped out of the doorway. Kenneth's apartment was huge. He'd lived in the building longer than Elahe but it still looked like he'd just moved in. It had been a long time since a woman had been here, loving him.

No woman loves you, I explained. Kenneth said: Thanks for that.

He showed me to his bedroom, where he'd been watching TV on the chaise. After he'd shut his computer, he lay down and folded his arms behind his head, as if he were a happy man without a care in the world. I sat on the edge of the bed and put my hand on his stomach. His shirt was rough.

Bibbs, why did you come here?

I unbuttoned one button so I could put my hand on his skin, but he was wearing an undershirt.

He tried to get up, but his abs couldn't manage without the support of his arms. 'Shall we go for a drink somewhere?'

I shook my head.

'OK, then I'll get you a drink here.'

He groaned as he got up from the daybed.

'Wait for me in the living room.'

Kenneth's apartment had two living rooms and three bathrooms. I sat down in the living room with the most furniture. Kenneth came out with two vodka sodas and sat beside me on the sofa.

'I'm so sorry about everything, Bibbs.'

I sipped my drink, wanting to say that I was, too, but for different reasons. What if I had let Sten call me Mummy, or if I hadn't drowned in Baby's emptiness. As if his emptiness had been a place where I could come into being. What if I'd been allowed to call him brother instead of darling. Because a brother is a brother, you can't stop being one. You can't unbrother no matter how fiercely you want to. It's different with darling. Fleeting. What if I hadn't met Mickey and what if Mickey hadn't seen something in me, which I understood was something that reminded him of himself. I put the drink down on the floor and Kenneth leapt up. Watch the floor! He put the glass on a newspaper. I moved closer to him. Kenneth mentioned the money, but he didn't need to remind me. I knew my debts. The walls of the room were glaringly empty, and I also knew what should go where and which

colours to choose. Kenneth's budget was different to the one
I'd been able to offer Baby, and Baby me. Kenneth was bab-
bling, clearly nervous. I took the drink from his hand and
winked at him as I placed it on the newspaper. Demonstrating
that we understood each other. On the sofa, I straddled his
narrow hips and ground into his crotch, and even though
I still felt sick, I tossed my blow-dried hair over my shoulders. I couldn't feel his cock. I took Kenneth's hands and put
them on my breasts, pulled down my shirt and bra. That's the
moment Baby died for.

'Bibbs.'

'Yes baby.'

'Bibbs, you've misunderstood.'

I stopped moving and he looked up at me.

'We're better as friends, you and I.'

'What do you mean, you said we'd have great kids
together?'

Kenneth pulled me down next to him. 'You don't even
want to have kids, Bibbs. I do in fact want more kids.'

'Why? You're never with the ones you already have.'

'I want another chance. I'll do it right this time.'

Maybe I want kids too, I said, as if in a dream being dreamt
by someone else. Kenneth ran his hand through what was left
of his hair. 'Baby's sad that you don't want any kids.'

The crown mouldings on the ceiling were beautifully
preserved.

'Well, I promised not to have an abortion if I get pregnant.'

Kenneth ran a hand through his hair again.

'No one gets pregnant just like that at your age, do they?'

I put my hands behind my head, like Kenneth had earlier.

'I might want to have a baby a little later on.'

Kenneth placed a hand on my belly.

'Happy thirty-ninth birthday, by the way.'

I put my hand on his hand.

'Thank you, darling.'

Kenneth stroked my skin.

'I have a present for you.'

He came back with a square package wrapped in brown paper, and I undid the satin ribbon. Inside was a notebook. 'To keep track of your debts,' he said. The gift was a joke.

'I mean, what do you get the girl who has everything?'

'I don't think I'm a girl anymore, Kenneth.'

'Did he really rape you?'

I sat up on the couch, my breasts still outside my shirt.

'Does it matter?'

Kenneth reached for my breasts, which were resting on my tummy.

'No, maybe not.'

Kenneth's debt was now paid, who cares for what.

Kenneth kept stroking my breast.

'Sorry, you might not want me talking about this while I'm touching you.'

'It's fine. It's all connected somehow anyway.'

I got dressed and said I had to go, and I did. He did nothing to stop me. But my leaving meant nothing but goodbye, so why should he have? It wasn't a gesture or blackmail. Talk to you later, we said to each other, and we meant it. I didn't want to go home yet. On the street, I took out my phone. I wrote to Sten. I wrote to Mickey and Texas. I wrote to Kenneth, even though we'd just said goodbye.

Lots of these men managed to bounce back after all kinds of accusations. The restaurant owner who raped a girl with a remote control was running a tapas place on Roslagsgatan. The artist who'd drugged a girlfriend of his and shoved his dick down her throat had thrown the most sought-after summer parties of the year. Those were the two examples freshest in mind. All other crimes were forgotten and if they were mentioned, the conversations died out. What was there to remember? Collectively, we made an effort to forget, that's the premise of existence, and it was too hard for people to think of a man both as someone they loved and as a criminal. Not for me, but I identified with the criminal. Where the women who had made such potent accusations had gone I didn't know. I smoked a cigarette in the bus shelter with the blue line under the ground, and consoled myself with this, on Baby's behalf. Baby didn't have much to lose. Not like I'd lost. And I wondered if Mickey had been wrong about that too; maybe getting gang-raped would have led nowhere. Mickey was over the hill and so was I. I called to ask him for advice, but he didn't answer. The ringing was a boatload of miles away. My 100,000 would get me Slipgatan back. Maybe.

The evening air was heavy. I hadn't admitted it to myself yet, but my disclosure didn't matter: I was defeated. I was already defeated when I stormed out of Slipgatan. My time had passed and those who were coming up behind me, ready to take my place, didn't know their history. They didn't know anything about Bibbs and everything that she had already done. Those who knew, like Kenneth and Sten, didn't want to know me, didn't want young women guessing their age. What had my plan been, a decade ago? I guess I didn't think I'd live this long. Who'd have thought it. Soon I wouldn't be able to get pregnant and claim that it was a slip. Bodil had made it through the window in the nick of time along with all those other whores, whereas I'd thought it was all going to take care of itself. Taxi drivers were leaning against their cars. There wouldn't be many fares tonight, but on Monday I was going to quit smoking, with or without Baby. Baby, who had been right about me not being able to afford Slipgatan on my own. I couldn't afford to live anywhere on my own. Stockholm was like the day or like he was, demanding everything and giving nothing. Not even high spirits. I went to the Theatre Grill, in shock or denial. Milli was sitting there, waiting. When I saw the people at the round bar, I picked up the phone. Sten had replied: 'Do not contact me.' I checked my account. The money was still there. I put the phone down on the table in front of Milli. My treat, I said to Milli, who was sitting on her own between two groups of quiet diners. Milli already had a drink, but I wanted to pay. She didn't like drugs, actually, she said, it's just that alcohol made her puffy. Let's go, she said, tapping one nostril with her index finger. I declined and she disappeared into the bathroom.

'No woman wants to be left at thirty-nine,' she said when she came back. I'd just been sitting there bolt upright, as if in a time warp. Thirty-nine? Who was she talking about?

'I was the one who left Baby,' I said. Then I said:

'I think Sten is interested in me.'

'At least we can rest easy in the knowledge that no one can walk all over us,' Milli said, her yellow silk blouse now creased at the armpits. I had the same blouse in my closet on Slipgatan.

'You and I could really be friends, Bibbs.'

The evening passed and at one point it looked like it might be a happy one. If I'd only wrapped my hand around happiness at just the right moment, I think I could have got it to stay. But I'm a romantic. Half would have been enough.

'You'll meet someone, Bibbs,' Milli offered, 'when this has all died down.' Wine glasses hung from the ceiling above the bar, like crystal chandeliers. It was the most beautiful thing I'd ever seen. Sometimes all there is to say is: Stockholm. You're beautiful.

'What do you mean died down?' I asked. I was jealous that Milli had the guts to do her nose, because it was a little button on her face whereas mine still had a human quality.

'Did Sten tell you that we used to be together?' I asked.

Milli burped.

'No.' I was trying to tell if she was lying.

'What, has Bodil never mentioned that Sten and I were together before they were? Because we were.' I knew Milli harboured a grudge, because weren't we all at some point.

'He has a totally sick mother fetish. Diapers and the whole shebang.'

Milli started tugging at her fingers.

'Sten was unfaithful the other year,' she finally said. Hungry for chaos and unable to keep quiet with the coke up her nose.

'He was? With who?'

'Someone who reported him to the police.' Milli said everything breezily, but I knew she knew that this was a forbidden conversation.

'What do you mean, who was she? Where is she now?'

'Like, dead.'

'No seriously, where is she?'

'I mean, she committed suicide.'

I shoved my chair back so forcefully that the people around us paused. I ordered three glasses of Riesling at the bar and downed one glass there, before turning around and carrying the other two over to Milli.

'So what's your take on Kenneth?'

Milli was scrolling on her phone.

'Kenneth is fried-4-life.'

'I mean Kenneth and me? Do you think we could be an item?'

Milli's eyelids had competing interests: open wide from the drugs or droop with the drink.

'You're too old for Kenneth.'

'I'm ten years younger than he is.'

Milli laughed heartily, like herself, and for the first time I liked her.

'Yeah, exactly. Way too old.'

In the early hours of Thursday morning, I woke up in Elahe's bedroom with a pain in my chest. The pain in my heart radiated. I pressed my hand against the ache, hard, to give it some pushback. My skull was bursting from the wine and I thought: It's breaking. The blind was pulled down, so for the first time this summer I found myself in the dark. 'Someone has to come and take this pain away from me,' I said, to hear what I sounded like. Then I said Baby's name, to hear what it sounded like. I was alone, again. Baby had taken me back to Hagaparken to see the blood moon. We walked side by side in the dark. I remembered where we were standing when we weren't seeing it. The nights were a pit to me. The mare, they call it, Marite said. Not an omen. Just an entity that belongs to the night. Baby became the pit's edge that I clung to when the mare turned up. As if I would disappear into the darkness if I didn't hold on. Desperation like a storm that we were frightened of. I cried for hours. There was no answer to the question why. The mare and the tears arrived after we'd been living on Slipgatan for six months. If there was an answer to the question why, it was too complicated. Not clean, like the truth. In those early Thursday hours, I missed Baby so much that I felt torn to pieces. Believe nothing else. You were so beautiful, but you had a wandering eye. You were a good fuck, I mean good-good. 'Don't leave me,' how many times did I beg you not to? 'If you leave me,' I said, 'I'll rob you. Stick 'em up, so I can wrap my arms around your waist.' I beat my chest and said his name. Melting down hurt, yes. Everything I did, I did for him. I dressed up for him, undressed for him. Ate food for him. Did the TV show for him. Said hello to the neighbour for him. Could make a comeback for him. Baby only had to do one thing and that was watch.

It was impossible to lie still in Elahe's bed. I wanted to beat the pain out of me. But I never saw the blood moon. Not sure what I was expecting either. That it would be a split blood orange, its red juice dripping down. Before the mare, during the nights of that happy summer, I was afraid Baby had contracted Lyme disease and checked him for ticks before we turned out the light. I'm sorry I said that you were a parasite on my joy. You weren't. You were my joy, my only joy. I just didn't know joy was this difficult.

That afternoon I decided to leave the bounds of the inner city. Yes, I wasn't myself. The leafy southern suburbs out the window looked like a fairy tale, apartments and detached houses, and men watching over their gardens, people impossible to imagine in a sincere way. The subway train was empty, as it usually was at this time of year.

'Now I know where I recognise you from. I just read your post.'

In front of me stood a woman whose features were centred in her face and everything was small except her presence, which was demanding and large, draining. I wanted to refuse her assertion, to say she was mistaken, but it was one of the few lies I could not truthfully tell.

'I read your post. You're brave.'

I'm sorry, I said submissively, because the rule is you have to be submissive, I'm sorry, I'd like to be left alone. The woman nodded, absolutely, and sat down two seats away but kept her eyes on me.

It was a cloudless day. We were still cockily waiting for the rain. The carriage was stuffy and I thought of money, friends, and ex-lovers. I wondered who these strangers thought I was. To shake off the woman, I looked down at my phone only to find my name looking back at me. I would transfer the money to Baby and write, 'I'm sorry.' I'm sorry, in the subject line of the bank transfer. Not the Slipgatan Money, that was mine, but the Baby Money. I was gonna get Baby Money. 'I'm sorry,' I'd write if there was room. This was the day I was turning thirty-nine. Elahe had called me in the morning to sing to me, and I kept quiet until she was done. I don't know anything about numerology and don't know what my destiny number is. Marite and I never got that far. But nine plus three is thirteen, it couldn't be good. She'd probably have told me: 'The unknown is not that one-dimensional.'

The train pulled in to the platform. The doors opened and the woman turned around right before I got out; I raised my hand in a wave. That wave cost me everything. The rule was that I had to be submissive, I repeated to myself.

The bulb was out on the third floor and when the old woman opened the door she was squinting, unsure of who I was.

'Do you recognise me?' I asked.

'Of course I recognise you.'

I pulled the door open and walked past her, while she stood behind me, perplexed, before her body started ticking along again. She shuffled past me, into the darkness. Newspapers and shoeboxes were stacked against the walls, rolled-up rugs leant on the furniture, and on the floor were lampshades without bases or lamp bases without shades. A freezer was stacked on top of another freezer that was stacked on top of another freezer and I walked over to the window and pulled up the blinds. The playground outside was quiet and the neighbours, usually noisy, were slow and listless, on their way home from a lake where they'd spent the day by the beach lying around like stewed snails.

She took a seat in the armchair and when I crouched down next to her, I was about to fall backwards, but grabbed the armrest. The hair on my thighs was golden but too fine for her to notice. Besides, her eyelids were shut. Her face evoked no sentimentality in me and through her thin arm ran blue-green veins, lighting her up from the inside. When I was a child, I used to look down her blouse at her large breasts, and there were warts growing around her nipples that were as large as her nipples themselves. When my mother told me to stop, Grandma would say, Let her be. Let her.

'Grandma.'
     I shook the armrest.
     'Grandma.'
     I shook her slender arm.
     'If it isn't Bibbs! So good to see you.'
     'Yes, I'm here to help you pay the rent.'
     She smelt of hard soap with a whiff of urine.
     'Pay the rent? Is it that time again?'

At the end of each month, I paid her bills and watered the plants. The plants were waiting to die, but I wouldn't let that happen and stuck my fingers into the nutrient-depleted soil, as if I knew what I was feeling for. Sometimes I cleaned the fridge or washed a load of laundry, depending on my mood. I got up and started looking for her iPad. Her friends in the sewing club got her to wish for one and it was a wish she never imagined would come true. Like when you say: 'I wish it wasn't so hot.' That's why it was a fun gift to give. A silverfish zipped across the table as I lifted a stack of advertising circulars and I swore but apologised before she had a chance to say anything. Grandma got up from the armchair and disappeared into the bedroom. Although no one had asked me to, I helped her with all sorts of things. I never complained or demanded anything in return. I had never asked for money and I had never, or rarely, cancelled our appointments at short notice. I needed money to be able to write 'I'm sorry' in the subject line of the bank transfer. Grandma thought it was good to be the first to say sorry. Pride doesn't serve love, Bibbs. That's how she'd put it, with concern, when we could still have a conversation. She shuffled towards me with the iPad under her arm, her faded flannel nightgown billowing over her gnarled feet.

'My pretty Elisabeth. I always watch you on TV.'

She patted me on the cheek and I took the tablet from her and helped her back into the armchair. Without waiting for her to drift off, I logged into her bank account using my social security number as a password. She had 30,000 in her savings account. If she'd had 130,000, I wouldn't have had to seek Kenneth out. Grandma's eyelids looked like sheets of pink gelatine. It was strange that she couldn't see through them. I didn't ask for anything in return, even though this apartment could sour a good mood. Besides, she never used the iPad I'd given her. Had I asked for the money she'd have said yes, but asking wasn't worth it. It was too complicated. I transferred 12,000 to my account. Grandma had fallen back asleep, breath shallow and rapid. The money was released immediately.

I put the iPad under the damp circulars on the table, no silver-fish in sight. I was struck by the impulse to clean, but I knew Grandma valued the circulars and the empty pots. These were her things.

'I'm going now,' I said out loud, to wake her up.

She looked up.

'If it isn't Bibbs! What are you doing here?'

'I stopped by to say hello. Mum says she'll be by tomor-row,' I said, kissing Grandma on the forehead. It was warmer in the stairwell than in the apartment. Before the door shut behind me, I heard her call out 'Send my regards to Baby.'

Mum didn't say happy birthday when I entered the bedroom. She said she'd seen me through the window and asked why I was limping.

'Nah, I'm not limping.'

Just like Grandma, she was going through a light-sensitive period and was lying in bed with the blinds down. Your mother is a seeker, Grandma said back when we could still talk, and this didn't escape me. My mother searched the cards, the moon and all kinds of stars. What was she looking for? I never bothered to ask.

'When I was your age, I had two kids,' she said, facing the wall. I almost didn't hear her, but I heard her.

'I know.'

'Have you been by Grandma's today?'

At Fridhemsplan, I had bought a tin of snus and the pouch under my lip was dripping. I took it out and instead of returning it to the tin, I kept the wet snus in my hand. My mother didn't smoke and today, on my thirty-ninth birthday, I'd been quitting smoking for nine years. Quitting was a verb. Something on-going. Sort of like a compulsive thought. There was no end to quitting, because it ended with you picking it back up again and then the quitting would start all over. Anyway I didn't smoke at my mother's because I didn't want her to feel bad. Kitte, our first family medium, had dental veneers and a Gucci Filofax. I didn't know what those two things meant, but I could tell they were important and so I wanted them too. Mum, Kitte had said, was an ice princess in a previous life. That was why she hated working. Grandma never cared if I smoked, but she didn't like the smell.

'How are you doing?' I asked my mother.

'Never ask anyone over seventy how they're doing.'

I went into the kitchen and shouted that I had been to Grandma's and she didn't recognise me. But it didn't make me sad anymore. Mum's kitchen cabinets were full of fast carbs and there was a whole shelf of diet soda in the fridge. When I came back into the bedroom with a glass of water she sat up, even though the bed's soft mattress was pulling her down.

'I thought you were gluten-free,' I said, handing her the glass.

'I understand that Baby has left you,' she replied and accepted it.

Mum never dried her hair after showering, and her hands with those long fingers of hers were freckled with age. Age spots, I once pointed out, but Mum said no, freckles are more chic. Her gel manicure was so grown out that the crescent of the nail bed was visible.

'No, he hasn't left me. I've left him.'

She sucked her teeth.

'How does Mickey feel about that, then?'

The sound coming from her mouth made me think of the crickets that had hopped through the door when Baby and I lived in the yellow house in Hagaparken, that happy summer.

'In time, you will reconsider the "happiness" of this summer,' Mum had said in the midst of that happy summer. Baby felt hurt by that statement, but I'd defended her. That's how she is, mired in loss. Every time we saw each other, she nagged me to see her again, and when I left, she said of course I was leaving. Even though I knew my mother was a Cassandra, I brought her prophecy for the happy summer to Marite. The crickets hopping through the window were not an omen, Marite had reassured me. Omens aren't particularly classical. Omens are signs that are impossible to catch sight of, which is why they're so threatening. Marite said that might sound stressful, and it was.

We had argued about the insects, Baby and I, because he kept nagging me to close the windows when we found crickets inside for the third time. He didn't like killing creatures. To me, it didn't matter if they were dead or alive, as long as they weren't alive in my house. I screamed when I discovered the crickets on the walls and inside the bedroom door, not bouncing but as calm as fat toads.

'Good,' Mum said when I didn't give her an answer to the question of what Mickey thought. 'I'm glad you left him. It's better to be the one to leave.'

I said I knew that.

'I know it's better.' She had fixed her gaze behind me and said good again. Her gaze was lost in her eyes. I fixed my eyes on her.

We gossiped about Baby and Mickey until she fell asleep and I kept myself from checking my phone. If the phone had been harder to catch sight of, I'd have taken the phone as an omen. But Marite said you couldn't take messengers for omens, because messengers were friends who'd got into someone else's trouble. From down on the street came the smell of flowers so fully in bloom they looked like they were one day shy of losing their petals. The day's heat had eased and softened their sweet perfume. No rain in sight. I bought a pack of cigarettes from the kiosk on the square. A fan was pointed out the door and I smoked my first of the day, while transferring Grandma's money to Baby. 'Sorry,' I wrote, instead of 'I'm sorry.' I didn't want to draw negative attention to myself. On my birthday a year ago, we'd gone back to Hagaparken in the middle of the night. This was the time we'd looked for the blood moon, but it was cloudy. We walked through the wilder parts of the park; the grass was wet with dew and the branches scratched us. I kept wondering what the moon would look like. The sweetness of the foliage cut through the cigarette smoke and I went down into the subway. Soon the scentless time would come. But first there was this time, first there was this.

Some women are not flames that burn through rock. Some women are a different kind of flame, an ordinary one. But not me, put me under the rock. I'll melt it. With this conviction, I returned to Slipgatan that Friday. Elahe's stairwell smelt of soft soap and the women cleaning stood against the walls to let me by. I was wearing new sandals. I had money in the bank. I was going to take what was rightfully mine. The taxi was waiting and when I slammed the door, the driver roared off into the intersection, as if his life depended on it. Someone shouted fucking maniac.

The air in the apartment was stuffy, hot, as if no one had been there all summer. But that's just how it felt. The day's mail was on the dresser in the hall, and Baby would leave it there from the time it arrived around 3 p.m. until after dinner, at 8 p.m. Then he'd take it into the kitchen to open it. He hadn't cleared away the make-up I'd left on the sink and I felt a tug at the hook attached to the thread running between my heart and Baby's. The bathroom looked the same as it did a week ago, but Nina had since looked at herself in the mirror here, and I rummaged through my brushes and sponges on the sink. There was a risk she'd used them on her face, so I threw them in the toilet and flushed. The handles whipped around in the water. I peed without wiping and flushed again, and one sponge went down but nothing else.

In the kitchen there were four bottles of wine on the sink, two of them empty, and I threw the unopened ones in the bin. Other than Baby having taken the photo from Elahe's wedding off the fridge, everything was the same, but I didn't need to have the photograph in front of me to see it. The photo was taken on Sveavägen and we were all dressed up. I was wearing a beige dress that Baby had given me after that vacation with Elahe when he'd hung up the phone on me every time we talked. Our faces were tense and relaxed in the picture. Mine was the tense one and his relaxed, because it was one of those nights when he'd taken up drinking again, and when the party was over he threw one of his shoes at me on Norr Mälarstrand. Baby had got a blister and I don't know why it made him angry, but even though I'd otherwise been irritable all evening, I was calm and languid. Before I had a chance to react, he took off his other shoe and ran away from me. I shouted but he didn't turn around. The Mälar Pavilion was adorned with colourful lights and I passed couples walking their bikes side by side, just to make the moment last a little longer. When I got back to Slipgatan, Baby was waiting for me on the stairs, blotchy around his eyes. Of course I forgave him. I always did.

I found the photo from the wedding in one of the kitchen drawers, right at the top, and I put it on the fridge. In the bedroom, the bed was made and the pillows were arranged on the thick coverlet, which I tore off. I removed the sheet and the rest of the bedclothes and went onto the balcony. The street below was empty. When I threw the material over the railing, I wanted it to look dramatic, like a sail, but it didn't. It looked like a lump.

When I opened my eyes, I saw someone I loved. The light was a shadow. I reached for Baby's cheek, but he recoiled. He was already talking when I woke up and sleep pulled me back in. I rolled onto my stomach. It was good to be home. But Baby wasn't about to let me rest after the long week. He took hold of my ankle and tried to drag me out of bed. I grabbed the edge of the bed and he pulled at me with all his might. Stubbornly I resisted and the bed slid away from the wall, but I stayed put. The legs of the bed groaned against the floor. We weren't saying anything, just sighing, stubborn, and the struggle didn't last long because suddenly Baby let go and turned to the wall where the print he'd given me as a three-year-anniversary present was hanging. It was the same print that Elahe had – a picture of a balcony door open onto a happy inner courtyard in another country. Baby pounded the wall with his fists and I counted ten blows. I stayed where I was, my body outstretched, as if he were still pulling, while I glanced over my shoulder without moving my head. My eyes hurt. Maybe we could be friends if we went back to

211

sleep. We'd resolved plenty of conflicts by falling asleep, in each other's arms. If I could fall asleep. Baby took the print down and held it over his head for what seemed like an eternity before he threw it across the room. I guessed the glass would break. I said to him with my face in the mattress, 'I guess the glass broke.'

There would be no more sleeping and my make-up would stain the mattress. I was wondering what to do when I heard a strange noise. I sat up. Baby was sitting on the floor. He was crying. Discomfort mixed with contempt as I saw the tears roll down his cheeks. What a pathetic man. Not resilient like Bibbs. His weeping was soft, but despairing. A sound only he could make, and Baby's face was open. His mouth too. I didn't know how to comfort him, because this was a different type of crying, and I sat down on the floor beside him.

'Bibbs,' he said, and my name was low in his throat. 'Bibbs, you have to leave.'

I shook my head, because I wanted him to trust me.

'Bibbs, you have to leave.'

I took the hair tie from around my wrist and put my hair up in a tight ponytail, drawing my eyes upward, awkward in the presence of this new Baby.

'Bibbs, I'm going to kill you if you don't leave.'

So kill me, I replied.

I'd selected every single item in this bedroom. The glass case where we kept our jewellery, the kitschy rosary that hung on his side of the bed, and the bedspread that was down in the courtyard. I had picked everything out, except the painting, which he gave me for our three-year anniversary. The yellow balcony. The picture of our happy summer.

Baby sat with his back against the wall, eyes closed, dully thumping his head on the wall, two two one, two two one. I was too hungry to wait for him to start talking. Where the painting had hung was a gouge in the plaster, next to the nail. We had nailed it wrong, while we were hanging it. It didn't matter. We were going to live here forever.

I went into the kitchen, opened the fridge. On the top shelf was a burrata. Baby always bought regular mozzarella so either someone else had bought the cheese or Baby had bought it to be someone else. I threw the cheese away and put a pot of water on the stove, went to the bathroom to wash the sleep off my face. I let the tap run so the water would get cold, took the brushes out of the toilet, and threw them in the bin. I washed my hands. I listened for Baby, but didn't hear him. Or that new sound. I took yellow concealer and dabbed it on the redness. I pulled down my panties and washed between my legs with a wet towel.

In the bedroom, Baby was still sitting on the floor, not crying.
    'I have to tell you something,' I said.
    His face did not confirm that he'd seen or heard me.
    'I have to tell you something, which I'm sure you'll want to hear.'

First off, I said, I know you've been cheating on me with Nina, and I waited a bit before continuing, to see if he would deny it. Instead, he looked straight at me, defiant. My disgust made me punch the bed. Baby said 'calm down' twice.

'Don't tell me to calm down,' I threatened. I threatened him, on Slipgatan. 'You said you thought she was ugly.'

My lips were dry and tasted of iron, of blood. Baby took his phone out of his jeans pocket.

'She's a fan, my fan. I know that all these years you've been mixing up who the fans belong to. So I want to take this opportunity, because there seems to have been some confusion. You don't have any fans. All the fans are my fans.'

He looked down at his phone. I thought, just die. My adrenaline was pumping.

'But that's not why I've come home.'

He put the phone down beside him, but kept looking at the screen. Baby had called me every day during my vacation with Elahe to tell me he didn't feel like talking to me.

'There's another thing I want to say.'

When he met me at Arlanda Airport, I asked him why and he said *because*.

'I lied.'

Finally he looked up from the screen.

'What I wrote to everyone. About you raping me. It was a lie.'

My throat was a small tube. Baby was about to say something but cut himself off and we sat quietly, listening to the neighbour take a piss standing up. After he'd flushed, Baby got up and went into the kitchen. The fridge opened and shut. I remembered the boiling water and went into the kitchen too, but Baby had already switched off the stove.

'Thanks for saying that, Bibbs, that's really good to hear.'

There's nothing that can't be undone, Baby used to comfort me when I felt tormented. I disagreed, but now that he was thanking me I thought that fruitless attempts to rewrite history had always been an annoying aspect of Baby's ethic, but for the first time this ethic could be used for good. Not just distorting the truth or taking back vicious words. Everything had been normal only a week ago and a week wasn't a long time. It wasn't too late for anything. He'd been unfaithful and I'd said that lie thing and I knew Marite would say that two wrongs don't make a right, but they don't *not* make a right. Marite was in favour of balance. Everything in the universe was about balance. My head felt light and I felt dizzy. 'Of course. I'm so glad. I wanted to talk to you about this, and then I wanted to talk to you about us, and about the apartment because—?'

'Unbelievable. You're not joking?'

'What?'

Baby was wearing his impossible face.

'You can't just break in here and tell me you're lying.'

First of all. First of all, I live here. So breaking in isn't a thing. Second, I explained, I'm trying to break a pattern. A pattern you usually criticise. I'm trying to take responsibility for my actions.

'I cannot believe you're making me explain this.'

I asked what he meant one more time. He'd backed me into the kitchen table. We were finally touching, his legs between mine and his face so close. Countless memories of his naked body twinged in my groin.

'What's more surprising than you playing dumb, is that I'm surprised you're playing dumb! But that's my fault. For letting you be the child in this relationship for four whole years.'

Baby liked to say that I'd grow out of it, though as we'd seen on TV, a person stops maturing at the age they become famous. You're not that famous, was Baby's point, and telling the truth was a sign of his maturity. He never thought of himself as a liar, rather as someone who presented various truths. But the absence of truth-telling was a habit that was hard to break, I explained to him. Someone asked when you got up and you said eight even though it was ten, another asked if you were going to meet up on Saturday and you said yes, even though the answer was no. Small lies, apparently insignificant, but altogether they placed a buffer between the person who told them and the world around. You got your peace and quiet at the cost of the world becoming distant. Desire was the easiest thing to lie about, because desire was the hardest thing to be honest about. Baby didn't know that the videos I liked best were the ones where the man was submissive and that I had never thought of submission as a fetish. No, I was searching for the tenderness, the look in the man's eyes as he lay with his head in the woman's lap, gazing up. How was the desire for tenderness different? It wasn't. So much had gone wrong between us, I thought; with Baby's body close to mine and the sudden scent of him, my anger

216

lost its focus. One of the things that had gone wrong was that I had never told him about my desire, and I no longer remembered the function of that specific lie. How ridiculous. The truth pointed to possibilities I didn't know existed.

'What I mean, Bibbs, is that you don't have to tell me that you lied. I know you've been lying. You've been lying about me.'

Other fantasies were harder to admit because they were arcane to me as well – why did I desire them? How could you admit to something that was a mystery to you?

'You wish I'd raped you, because in your disturbed mind, rape means someone wants you.'

I wanted to put the water back on. I was hungry. But he was so close, I also wanted to stay right here. I said I'm sorry, what more can I do. I'm sorry. Baby called every day on my vacation with Elahe just to hang up.

'My boss wants a meeting with me, otherwise no one has got in touch. Just a bunch of mentally ill cunts who wrote to tell me that I'm dead. Murder threats, Bibbs. Understand? And not a single friend. I've called everyone, not even Mickey, not even Kenneth, who himself. . . and I haven't even done anything.'

His voice broke.

'You're aware that Mickey isn't your friend, he's my colleague,' I said, trying to help.

Baby started crying again, saying 'why' in various ways. Up close, his face was hard to get a grip on and the blue under his eyes was tending towards green with hints of yellow. My thoughts were amorphous like the memory of a dream. In that moment, I didn't know why I had said what I had said. It was a desire hidden from me and therefore difficult to be honest about. I don't know why. *Because*? Baby's intensity troubled me.

'Did you see my apology?' I asked.

Baby lost the thread of his lament.

'I transferred 12,000 to you. That's not apartment money, it's just for you. Maybe you didn't see? But I wanted to give you something nice, so you'd know how sincere I am. That my apology is sincere.'

Baby put his hand over his mouth as if to hide a smile, but the smile never appeared. I used to count his teeth with my index finger. Sometimes their surface was slick in a way that would cause my finger to slip. What more can I do, I said. I'm sorry. It's not like you're famous. Nobody cares if you raped someone or not, the only thing they care about is if I was raped. And I have been! By the way, you cheated. With a CHILD. Nobody knows who you are. You threw me out. You promised never to leave me and then you left me.

Baby grabbed my chin roughly and said:

'Listen.' His nails were bitten down and his cuticles were jutting out like stiff splinters. 'I don't want you. The thought of fucking you makes me sick. Do you understand? You've ruined my life. You're a psycho bitch. Nonetheless, and never forget, I don't even want to rape you.'

Baby melted into me, or entwined with me, and pressed his crotch against my leg and I felt his erection. I used to worship his dick, which was more long than wide, and he didn't shave, nor did he groom. I teased him for being from the Seventies and I used to take his glans in my mouth and suck on it gently, with a loving tongue, and slowly draw back the foreskin with my lips as the tip entered my throat. He said my mouth was so hot it burnt. I was the flame, or was it him. One of us was the stone. A sort of reciprocal action, but I tired of oral sex. As one does. His glans was deep red, like real meat with blood. I wanted the intimacy and touched my finger to the cracks in his foreskin like I did his teeth and said: 'There's the herpes that you claim is latent,' but he maintained that he'd had no idea. I'm sure that was true. Baby didn't know anything about his body or his soul. When I met his ex at a bar, she said: 'So now you have herpes too!' And those insignificant blisters moved through Stockholm like a map of Baby's hysterical nights; now they had reached Nina. So he lied. So did I. Who cares. It made me folksy. Baby's lies were hard to get a handle on, because they were about making me doubt myself, not believe him. I was brilliant until I wasn't, but I forgave him and I understood what he meant about me thinking rape was courtship. One strategy I developed as a child was to construct erotic fantasies about being attacked because if I was horny when I was being raped, it wasn't rape. This meant I couldn't be raped and it was still better to be raped than to be left. Being left is the worst of all. Rape is like sex. Identical in execution, but the feeling is different and I had made that feeling mine. So rape me, or beat me. As long as you don't leave me. Baby was wrong about it being sick to feel that way. I'm sure it's very common. Mickey thought so too. Bodil, everybody. It was all noise anyway. It was all

noise surrounding the flame that could burn through stone.
Had Baby been a person who could understand I would have
explained, but he was stupid-stupid, a stupidity I loved. A
stupidity that, like the lie, created space for me, because he
wasn't smart enough to mirror me, or see me. Instead of
explaining myself, I put my arms around his neck.

'Believe me when I say I've been longing for you,' I said,
pressing my mouth to his white T-shirt, and through the
fabric was that slender chest, and my breath was hot. It made
the fabric damp. I unfastened the belt of his black jeans and
Baby pulled them down. We'd done this before. He felt my
pussy with one hand and sighed when he felt how wet I was.
The wetness came from my heart. The wetness was the truest
thing. Baby gently put his other hand around the back of my
neck, and the hair that hadn't found its way into my ponytail was curly. It was hot outside and it was hot inside. As it
always was, unless I was misremembering. Were there days
with fresh, clear air? No, there couldn't be. Were there days
without leaves on the trees? I sat down on the kitchen table
and pulled my panties aside, impatient. When he slid his dick
inside me, he said my name.

'Don't say Bibbs,' I reminded him, 'say brother,' but
before we could say anything else, he had torn himself from
my arms.

'You have to leave, Bibbs.' On wet, horny legs, I got down
off the kitchen table.

'I'm serious,' he said, 'leave,' and then he turned to the
sink and grabbed a wooden spoon and slammed it into the

counter until it cracked. Then he grabbed a ladle, made of steel, and hit the stove until it bent. The ladle looked like a big fish hook. Baby's pale bottom had dark hair that sprouted from between his buttocks like a fan. He grabbed the dish rack full of washed dishes and slammed it into the sink.

'Do you have to be so dramatic,' I said, pulling up my panties. 'Please don't fly off the handle like that,' I continued as I walked into the hallway, not afraid but. Baby hated it when I said 'please', thought I was being haughty. He came after me, but stumbled over his jeans and grabbed the coat rack for support. They all fell to the floor.

'Admit that I never raped you!' He screamed and was a ridiculous sight, there on the pile of jackets, but fit to burst, he got up and pulled his jeans up. The open belt lolled like two tongues on either side of his fly.

'Admit that I never fucking raped you,' and I screamed back:

'BUT I ALREADY DID.'

Baby's eyes changed. Any woman who lives with a crazy man knows that when his eyes change, it's time to back off. It's like you accidentally flick his switch. And once you've flicked it, you can no longer control him. You push with all your might against the bad stuff, but only until he switches, that's when you turn and run. You run as fast as your legs can carry you, because when a mad man accelerates, it's the end of hard against hard. The switch reveals an inescapable truth, and it's that he's the hard one and the other person is fragile. The other one is me, I'm fragile. I lowered my voice to show that I wasn't challenging him. To show that I was obeying the switch.

'Darling, I already did.'

I put my hands in the air. Surrendered, both palms turned to the ceiling as if to say: Take everything. Someone rang the doorbell. We both turned around.

Fat Nina from Örkelljunga was on the other side of the door with her expensive strawberry hair.

'What do you want?' I asked, blocking the doorway before she could say anything. I didn't want her to see Baby. But Baby was standing close behind me, peering over my shoulder.

'Bibbs is just leaving.' I felt sick.

'I just got here.'

Baby said: 'You've been here long enough.'

Nina looked embarrassed. Like she was going to cry.

'What do you have to cry about?' I asked. She started crying. I couldn't fucking believe it. I rolled my eyes.

'Don't roll your eyes,' said Baby, who had pushed me out of the doorway and planted himself between us.

'I'm not rolling my eyes at you.'

Nina rubbed her eyes.

'Bibbs, I didn't mean to. . . I didn't know you were here. I hate making people sad. I'm sorry. Maybe I'd better go.'

'This is my apartment,' I said, 'so yeah, it's probably best.'

Baby said: This is not your apartment.

'If you'd listened to me instead of getting all hysterical,' (I felt brave again because Nina's presence meant refuge from his dangerous anger), 'you'd know I have the money. The apartment, as you promised, is mine.'

Nina's idiot face and Baby's ability to control himself in its presence deflated my announcement. She didn't seem to understand what I was talking about and he didn't seem to think the money meant anything. The self-consciousness of having completed something you'd taken on washed over me and the triumph failed to materialise. I had overdone it, I thought, when I saw the two empty shells in front of me. The hall floor was laminate. Nina was bloated. Baby shallow. Not worthy of my grand show. Something in Baby's face also told me that he hadn't been serious about the money. It was Friday. Fridays are EuroJackpot days, but I didn't have a ticket and so had no chance of winning. Rent was due soon and my last credit card was about to max out. To the best of our ability, we had tried to build a normal life here, a life for two normal idiots, but faced with my man and his lover, 100,000 sounded like pennies. So what? they thought. So did I. The thing about money is that as soon as it's sorted, you have to sort out more. One payment is not enough. I was ready to admit defeat, but the admission didn't hurt because the admission came with certainty. There was no Slipgatan without Baby.

'OK fine. If you're not leaving, Bibbs, then we will,' Baby said, fastening his belt. 'But keep your hundred grand. We'll talk about this later.'

Nina was trying not to look at his open jeans. I gave a hacking laugh. Haha. She wasn't ready for this life.

'You're not ready for my life.'

Nina muttered. Baby knew I hated it when people mumbled.

'I don't want your life,' I heard under her breath.

'It's not all about you, Bibbs,' Baby said, and I knew he was right, but this was about me.

'I made you,' I said, to both of them. Baby repeated that it was up to me which one of us would leave. What kind of choice was that. The violence in him had settled and he was a different man now. I knew which one. Fake-Baby. At first he was Fake-Baby with me, when we thought we could be new people with each other. When we thought everything that had come before didn't matter, and when dishonesty was still wrapped around us like a protective seal. No one demands truth from those newly in love. On the contrary, truth is rejected.

'Before you go,' Baby said, making the decision that I would be the one to leave, 'will you tell Nina what you told me?'

I said I didn't know what he was talking about. The switch in Crazy-Baby's pupil had been flicked.

I said, OK fine. Baby didn't rape me. There. Now go suck each other's cocks or whatever it is you're gonna do. Nina cried out. An oh escaped her tongue.

'I knew it!' Did you really. How long have you been sleeping together, I asked, since we're being honest with each other?

'You don't have to answer that,' Baby said in a command-
ing tone. I knew they hadn't been sleeping together for long,
otherwise Nina would have looked dissatisfied. She was wearing a long dress in a ditzy floral pattern with puffy arms and
I couldn't tell if she was dressing like that in order to perform
girlishness or because she was still so close to childhood that
it wasn't weird. Her shoes were made of cloth. Her purse
wicker. I saw what Baby saw and he wasn't seeing Nina.
Fuck Nina. Baby, I think I know you. I think I know you
better than you know yourself. Her youth was his chance
for a do-over. To give Fake-Baby another try, and this time
he might stick. Maybe even outstrip the real Baby. Not have
to go back to himself. Newfound fame, which was so shiny
(until it wasn't anymore). Around Nina's wrists were home-
made bracelets with colourful plastic beads, and I thought:
'Baby, I wasn't the one who wanted the lies. That was you.'
There was none of Fake-Baby left between us. I'd seen and
heard too much. I'd seen and heard it all. The truth annihi-
lated him. I realised this when I saw the freckles on her chest,
how unbothered she was about sun-damage and wrinkles.
There he would rest as if he were a different person, for a
time. Maybe part of me sympathised with him, but I'd never
be offered a comparable chance. And Baby and I kept track of
everything and traded one injustice for another. People like
me didn't get a do-over. I couldn't pretend that the years that
lay behind me had nothing to do with me. That was a dream
so unattainable it couldn't be dreamt.

'You two are pathetic,' I said. 'Ridiculous. You deserve each other.' I put on my sandals. Nina had gained ground and was now in the hall. In the heart of the hall. She took off her ugly handbag, which she'd been wearing as a cross-body, and put it on the rattan chair.

'How much do you weigh?' I asked. 'You know Baby has a fat girl fetish?'

'Shut your mouth, Bibbs,' Baby said. Everything was slipping through my fingers. I didn't know how to close my hand. Nor could I stop the slippage.

'How much do *you* weigh?' she asked. She slyly narrowed her eyes.

I'd been eating poorly all week and the tears that came surprised me. The ache in my eyes stopped. A piece of cartilage in my chest that was connected to the tear duct had come loose and the tears were pouring out with such force that I couldn't shove the cartilage back in place. To get a hold of myself, I bent down and pretended to adjust the buckles on my sandals. Tears on my foot.

'I'm pregnant,' I said, straightening up.

'If you think I look bigger than usual, it's because I'm pregnant,' and Nina's sense of belonging to Slipgatan left her. I saw it happen. Baby was standing behind me. He made a sound. I didn't recognise it, but it wasn't that crying sound. If I turned around, he'd see my tears, and I wasn't going to give him that. I'd probably put on weight during the week, Nina was right. One short week ago I'd been managing my carbs well, eating kale salad, and drinking vodka soda. Tears streamed down my face.

Nina said:

'Oh, my God.'

Yes, oh my God. Why did I come back home? Was it to lose it all or to win it all back? It was to win it all back.

At the foot of the stairwell the front door opened and the door behind Nina blew open. On Slipgatan, the door had to be shut tightly and I was in the stairwell catching hold of the handle when Yvonne, the woman who lived in the apartment next to us, approached. We had the same star sign and she was about to turn seventy.

'Bibbs! I think your laundry blew off the balcony.'

I said no, not our laundry, then remembered the bedding, and started to close the door as she hurried up the stairs.

'Well, there's a whole pile of bedding on the ground down there, you'd better pick it up before it gets too dirty.'

I thanked her, but Yvonne wasn't finished. 'Belated congratulations, by the way!'

Yvonne had always found Baby to be very handsome and was thrilled when I lost weight. She had two daughters and asked me about once a month when Baby and I were going to have a baby. 'Don't wait too long,' she had warned, as if she knew something about the future about which I had no idea. After a year of living on Slipgatan, I got pregnant, but

I struggled to tell Yvonne. I'd tried, but changed my mind. The second Baby came inside me I felt it stick, and I knew I was pregnant. We hadn't talked about becoming parents, but he had sex with me like he was longing for something, like he wanted to tie me up, and my pussy was drawing him in, biologically. The day after my period was due, I took a pregnancy test while Baby was lying on the bed and when I came into the bedroom and told him I was pregnant, he said: 'Fucking shit,' for which he later apologised. Baby really wanted to be a father, but was sure he would be bad at it. I believed him and when I saw the plus on the stick material-ise I was absolutely sure that I didn't want to bind myself to Baby. My body had told me what my heart wasn't ready to hear, which was that our happy summer had come to an end.

I was pregnant for six weeks and when no one was looking I put my hand on my belly to see what it was like. I had the abortion at Marite's house, who treated me to fried shrimp with sweet-and-sour sauce. I was thirty-six and was sure there would be other chances. Baby punched himself in the face when we argued on the night I was bleeding the most. 'Promise me you'll never have another abortion!' he shouted and I promised.

Yvonne had children and a career and a nice husband who liked to travel. She caught sight of Baby and Nina. 'I recog-nise you!'

'Yvonne.' I wanted to push Nina out of view or tell Yvonne she was wrong, this young woman wasn't Nina at all, but some ordinary, mediocre girl. No one special.

'Yvonne, we were in the middle of something here.'

'It's you, you're so very talented! Nina Samuelsson!'

Nina was too weak to resist.

'You really think so?'

'I just saw you on SVT Play! Such great fun! You know, the two of you actually look a bit alike,' Yvonne said, and it was meant as a compliment to me.

'Thank you,' I said. Yvonne was resting her hand on the door frame and I wanted to slam the door shut.

'We were in the middle of something here, so.'

My voice was stressed and Yvonne lost her thread. She looked at us one at a time, probing or critical.

'Somebody needs to go downstairs and pick up the laundry,' she said and Nina said I can do it and I said OK, but Baby said no I'll do it and put on his shoes and shut the door behind him. I heard his and Yvonne's voices echoing in the stairwell.

Nina was blushing from neck to forehead and shaking her head incredulously.

'And there we were, talking about children at Tennstopet. But you couldn't have known that you were pregnant then, or did you? I guess those nights are over, nights like the one we had. All for the best, I suppose.'

She wanted to be a mother one day, too, as she'd said during our conversation the other night, still searching for commonalities. But a young one! Women had to take care of each other, she thought. . . no, she *knew*. Only a woman can understand another woman. What it's *really* like. Nina wanted to be a sister. Nina wanted to make a positive contribution to the world. Not a negative one. She'd failed at that, she admitted. I could hear that her girlishness wasn't put on. Her girlishness was a lingering idiocy. Something that hadn't been broken yet. Perhaps something that she had been spared. Her round face, the minimal make up. 'All women are my sisters,' she said, visibly moved by the gravity of the moment. 'When a child is involved. . .' She was crying again. 'I'm sorry, I just feel so fucking stupid.'

I wondered if she understood that she was the child in this situation.

One afternoon Nina had got a call from an unknown number. The man on the phone had been given her number by a mutual friend and said that he'd seen Nina at the grocery store and thought she was beautiful; he then asked her out. Nina was flattered. They met at a strange restaurant. Upon meeting, she said, she realised that she recognised the man. It was Baby, Bibbs's boyfriend. At first Nina had been uncomfortable and was about to get angry, but Baby had said the relationship was basically over. Baby had been clear. Everything was settled. Bibbs and Baby's future was written, as was Nina and Baby's. Nina was just a girl who wanted a guy who wanted to be with her. I could see it wasn't an act. Nina wasn't used to men being that determined. Men her age were hard to get hold of and they never called. They barely texted. Furthermore, Baby had told her that I was hard to live with and that Baby wanted to start a family. But I didn't want to; no, I flat out refused and had gone through with an abortion without consulting him. Nina tried to verify the claim but I didn't respond. The moment Baby laid eyes on Nina, she continued, he knew that the two of them could have something special. Nina thought she was going to leave, but they ordered drink after drink and went back to her place together. Sorry. She'd never thought of herself as the younger woman, or the other woman. Nina thought those were sexist tropes, by the way. They'd been dating for just over a month, and when we ran into each other at Tennstopet, she could no longer ignore the fact that what she'd done was not sisterly. After all, I was a real person and she was drunk and knew that Baby had left me. Baby had written to her that today was the day. He had even proposed to Nina on their first date. I thought back to the first time he called me and screamed: 'I love you.' At the time, I didn't even know his last name. Baby proposed to women when he was that abysmal type of drunk, desperate. Desperate and scared and unwilling to be the person he was.

When Nina told me about the proposal, I was alarmed, in spite of myself. I wondered how long it had been since he stopped feeling the thread attached to the hook tugging at his heart. I wondered how long he'd felt abandoned. Nina tried to confess to me that night at Tennstopet, but it was hard to find the words. So she dragged it out. She invited me home to tell me. The toilet tended to be difficult, she said by way of wrapping up her story, you have to wait for it to stop running, then you can flush again.

'I don't want to come between you,' Nina said. 'Or your family. Baby isn't even. . . He's not my type of. That world is too. That world is not for me.'

233

The world I shared with Baby, where we'd been fused together in the fire, a fire of heartbreak and grief. I had always been right about Baby, that he would betray me. I could trust myself.

'He's a fan,' I said. Nina smiled the way weak women smile. Nothing about her was honest.

'Yeah,' she said, 'a fucking groupie.'

'But now I'm going to have a baby with that groupie,' I said. She said, of course, sorry. I didn't mean it.

'So he's who you got herpes from,' I said.

'Baby said he didn't know he had it,' she said. 'I guess it's latent in some people.'

Once she'd said it out loud, it stopped being true. I nodded. The doorbell rang. Baby was back with the bedding in his arms and Nina grabbed her bag off the chair. He said:

'What the hell, Bibbs.' With the bedding in his arms. There was grass on the sheets in his arms. He sounded a little angry.

'I guess I'll be going then,' she said like a question, and for a moment I was afraid Baby would stop her, but he said, 'Yeah, I guess you better.'

Anger flashed in her childlike face, but I was the only one who noticed. Only women know, I thought. Halfway out the door, she turned around to say:

'Talk to you later,' and I echoed, 'Talk to you later.'

The storm in Baby had settled and his body felt supple in my arms. I had underestimated the crisis. I had underestimated the intensity with which he wanted to abandon himself.

'Darling, are you pregnant?' he said, and his eyes were frightened and his mouth angry and his voice in love. He held my face between his hands.

'How the hell are we going to do this?' But he wasn't asking me. He was asking some higher power. We kissed. Out of the corner of my eye, I saw the overturned coat rack. Baby said he didn't know what to say, but then said, You have to stop watching porn with pregnant women. We kissed again.

'We can make porn with pregnant women now,' I said to console myself. Baby took me by the hand and led me into the living room and we sat on the couch. The plant I didn't know the name of, by the window. Baby said we were going to be happy. We were going to be happy. Baby asked how long I'd known. I didn't answer. He looked tired. For me, lying had always been an intention. An intended truth.

'There's no one like you,' Baby kept repeating. Like a curse that would not lift. I rode him on the sofa. When he was close, I told him to come inside me and tried to sense if it stuck. I wanted to imagine that it did. When a lie steps into the truth, it dissolves and disappears.

The peachy evening light was a caress outside the window, and reminded me of the fruit growing in the garden, before we knew each other. Before we knew that we fit together like a knife in the flesh. Through the living-room window I saw the leaves moving pleasantly, caressing the evening in turn. As if the evening were something you caressed yourself into. Baby lay with his head in my arms, looking up. That's what it looked like, true intimacy. What I'd been searching for. His forehead was smooth and his eyes were sad.

'I'm glad we got rid of her,' I said, playing with his hair. I don't know if I was thinking about it in the right way, but I thought this true intimacy had nothing to do with the pregnancy, but with the truth.

So I said: 'I'm not really pregnant.' Baby didn't say anything. I said: 'Or rather I'm probably not pregnant. I don't know for sure. It felt like something stuck.'

'What.'

I tried to hold him in place in my lap, but he squirmed.

'But I really do have the money,' I said, trying to sound happy.

I really do have the 100,000 I said I'd sort out.

I wanted Nina to go.

I want to be pregnant.

I'm crazy about you.

I want you to get me pregnant.

I want you to forgive me.

I want you to come inside me when you lift my legs above my head,

and hold my feet.

Don't leave me.

I forgive you.

Nina said you proposed.

You proposed to me first.

I'm proposing to you now.

There's no one like me, you said so yourself.

I'll let you be what you are.

Nina is too young, too happy.

Heart kin.

We're psycho kin.

I've given you everything. I mean everything-everything.

I have nothing else.

I have no one else.

I bought two of this very table,

and I kept listing the wrongs I'd forgiven, and gifts I'd given, and Baby listened. Bad finances were like negative sway or minus sway, but my investment in the market of grace was sound. I had forgiven everything and everyone. When Baby said: 'I hate you,' I answered: 'But I love you.' When they accused me of selling out, I agreed. When I lost jobs to younger people, I said be my guest, and I'd forgiven everyone without difficulty because I knew there was no redress to be had. Redress is false. That had been cemented this week. All that exist are the days and the money and the ways both can be spent. Marite argued that forgiveness was a lie, if you kept score like I did. I didn't keep score to be petty. I did it so I could one day mortgage a thousand wrongs for one massive one. Tonight was that night.

'Do you have the money?' he said, perhaps relieved not to have to be the bad father today. Perhaps surprised to find out the difference between wants and needs.

'Yes, as I told you last week, I have the money.'

'Can't you just be honest with me, Bibbs. There's no point in us lying to each other anymore.' I realised Baby was right. We'd started down the path of truth, which is where we'd been heading anyway. Because we'd seen each other in full glare all those many times. But now the truth would also be spoken, not just revealed. No more Fake-Baby and no more Fake-Bibbs. In my case, that meant he knew that a lie was as easy to come by as the truth.

'OK, I didn't have the money when I said I did. But I have it now. I sorted it out so that you'd see that I could.'

'You said I raped you and until one minute ago you were pregnant. Why should I believe that you have the money?'

'I love you,' I said. 'I have the money. You can either take it or we can, we can do something else with it. Nobody wants you as much as I do.'

Baby I'll stop being me for you.

Baby had his thinking face on.

'Did you do all this to get me back?' he asked. I nodded, thinking it would be my final lie. Baby said: 'Oh baby,' as if he were horny. He probably was horny. He always wanted to be in the light, but not in its harsh full white glare. In the warm flattering light.

'I want to stop lying,' I said. 'I want you to love me.'

'Of course I love you,' Baby said. And straight out into the room he said: 'I guess it's just you and me.' I knew what he was feeling; the secret had bound us more tightly.

'The last time you got pregnant, you promised me you'd never have an abortion again, if it happened.'

I took his hand and put it on my stomach, as if I already were pregnant.

'I promise not to have an abortion.'

DAYS & DAYS & DAYS

'Don't touch me,' he said as my hand found its way under his sweater, but then changed his mind.

'Yes, do touch me. I've done so many stupid things too,' he confessed.

I said, Yes. You've done a lot of stupid things. I forgive you everything.

'I know, Bibbs,' Baby said.

We had dinner and I ate sitting on his lap. It was playing at girlishness. Him with his arm around my waist. Side by side we performed our evening routines and while I hung up the picture with the cracked glass, Baby made the bed with fresh sheets. As we settled into bed, Baby whispered that he also wanted me to get pregnant. It didn't feel like he belonged to me anymore, after he'd been inside Nina. It felt like he was dirty or used up, but we slept together again. Nina and I were the truth of Baby's desires. I wished I didn't know. If fat was what he wanted, I was either fat or undesirable. 'Maybe you're pregnant now,' he whispered. We hadn't had this much sex in over a year. The blinds were down and we knew each other better in the dark than in the light. I was thirty-nine years old. Baby hadn't wished me happy birthday.

'Tomorrow you can issue a correction or something, say we're friends again, maybe say the hormones made you crazy or something. You can say you're pregnant if you're going to be anyway.'

I turned my back on him and he came closer. We knew we were each other's hostage.

'I promise I will.'

'What's on your mind?' he asked.

'Nothing.'

But I was wondering what Mickey and the others would say.

Maybe I'd have to get another job. Or worse. A child. To get myself out of this jam. My throat felt tight. Everyone would be yelling at me and writing about this. Everyone was so many people and Baby was just one person, and Kenneth would certainly want his money back. I tried to say something about how I had come into possession of the money, but I had trouble finding the words and Baby hadn't asked. Now I thought he probably didn't want to know. Baby fell asleep first. I tried not to let that hurt me.

One day, everyone we know will be dead. This will be true for one of us and it's a loneliness we must bear. Baby thought this was a ridiculous way to put things into perspective.

OK, but one desire is to rise above one's desires and another desire is to let go, and now I was letting go. He didn't understand what I meant by that either.

'After everything else has been consumed something has to be left that's MINE and mine alone. The lie can be seen as a form of. . . silence.' I'm not accountable to the world, Baby taught me. He used to say that to me when he came home at night and I asked where he'd been.

Baby pulled up the blinds. His tattooed body was thinner or was mine larger. That big diagonal scar from an operation in his teens ran across his stomach. The tattoo across his chest was of a dragon, done the same day as his sister's high school graduation. On the same evening he'd walked into the road without looking and was hit by a car. Other people's achievements always made him feel worthless.

'What is there to confess, really?' I asked him. 'My life is not a crime. Women's lives are not a crime. And haven't we agreed that I've taken out a mortgage on your forgiveness and now we're friends again.'

Annoyed, Baby said, 'Just write that I haven't done anything to you.'

'Why don't you post about it yourself if it's that important to you?'

'I don't even have a fucking hundred followers, Bibbs, and denying a crime isn't the same thing as taking back an accusation.'

'It's not my fault you don't have any followers,' I said, scrolling through the photos in my phone. There was no image that went with what Baby wanted me to write, so instead I started a draft in my Notes app. 'I lied.' No. No one wants to listen to everything that exists between two poles. I switched my screen off. The movements he made in the bedroom were familiar, as if he'd stolen them from me. Anyone who lets contempt for their lover coexist with love remembers the incident that cracked their idealised image. For me, it was that time in the taxi when Baby was so drunk he farted. Later that night, he told me I was a classic beauty. The assertion hurt me. I was not a classic beauty. Nor did I have to be.

Baby went into the bathroom and turned on the shower. When he came back into the bedroom, I was already getting dressed. 'Where are you going?' he asked. To pick up breakfast, honey, and I grabbed my bag, which was in the hallway.

As I was putting a pair of clean panties in the bag, I thought again, what crime am I guilty of? I did what everyone wanted me to do. I said what they were dying to hear. Yes, I'm a fucking nobody and a person had really done things to my body. Put stuff in it. They loved knowing that and when they saw us they thought we were defenceless and naked, and they jerked off to it. Baby and I had let each other down in different ways, all the thousands of emails he never replied to, for example. All the times he turned around and asked how I was doing. We did truly-truly love each other in the night-night. Whereas in the day. Whereas furniture and garlic braids. The problem was that I lacked the routine that the nine-to-five provides, the routine couples rely on. You weave a life of shared activity. Please stop asking me how I'm doing, I wanted to say each time he came home from work. The question hurt me. He should have known. Baby was the first person I knew who expected something from me, money, an invitation, an idea, and this expectation became the direction of life, my gravity. So I shaved my legs in the bath, regularly, to be a girlfriend. Sometimes I shaved too hastily and a drop of blood would seep out and mix with the water. Before the drop dissolved, it looked like smoke. I stopped smoking too. I gave everything-everything. From the drawer, I grabbed a couple more pairs of panties, just in case.

Baby was heading for the shower, but I stopped him.

'What is it, Bibbs?'

'I'm just sad, it is what it is.'

He didn't close the bathroom door before he walked under the stream of water. I packed the make-up that was loose in the bedroom dresser. In the past, I had always returned, but then I wasn't sneaking out. When I walked along the water last winter and saw smoke rising from the ice with no apparent explanation, I pretended for a moment that I wasn't going to go back home. 'How beautiful,' I'd say to myself, in that distilled darkness. But then I went back, to Slipgatan, and left pride to those who had a use for it.

'Come here,' Baby would say each time he greeted me at the door, and I knew it was true. I was welcome there. I don't know how to explain what I was good at that made me welcome there. I was good at seeming happy.

'See you soon,' I called to Baby, my voice pained. Through the water, he couldn't hear the nuances. Goodbye to my Baby, who I loved so much. The door slammed behind me and I hadn't taken my keys. It didn't matter. The lie I'd told my friends, that I was the one who'd left him, had always been an intention. Long before he left me, I'd decided to do the same. I didn't have an envelope of cash to put on the kitchen table, but if I had, I would have obviously texted, 'Thank you for our time together. It's over.' With this, the lie stepped into truth and dissolved.

We, the mad and homeless, loitered outside the 7-Eleven. I asked for a cigarette and got one. Am I ugly, I had asked Baby before I left, and he had kissed me, through the streams of water. Yes, darling. 'Careful, you'll get wet.' I bought a coffee and a sandwich roll. The morning was posing, super-ficial and on the benches the poor slumped alongside the rich. At the pharmacy by the subway entrance, I bought a morning-after pill and washed it down with my coffee while standing outside. My business model was founded on one thing above all, and that was my credibility. The fact that it was possible to believe that I was who I said I was. Bibbs had to mean something. Bibbs meant being young and unboth-ered, like a remnant from the Nineties. Bibbs didn't mean babies and humble apologies. I went down into the subway and warm winds blew through the tunnel, whipping my hair into my face. My currency wasn't credibility alone, it was also familiarity. I was beloved for confessing my crimes as I was committing them. The problem was that confession and credibility were in direct conflict with each other and no one would understand this. So I had to choose between the two. The choice was carefully calculated, nothing personal. Mathematics.

In the beginning, Baby had called me Norma Jean. He said it was Marilyn Monroe's real name. My guess is that he thought he had access to my real name. He posted pictures of me and wrote 'Norma Jean' under the picture. I was standing on a balcony in Lisbon, thinking he loved Bibbs when he took the picture. Steep houses in the background and climbing plants. Norma Jean, I mouthed to myself in the cold Portugal water. Baby was slim on the rocky beach, and the waves were rough. He waved. I was smiling with my whole face even there, in the water, when he wasn't looking, in love by day, but lying awake at night. My name was not Norma Jean. Any real woman was no more than the faded image of a fake woman, unfortunately.

The subway train pulled into the platform and the phone rang. I answered it without boarding the train. It was Mickey, who would be back soon, and then we would make a five-year plan. Could I start blogging again? he asked. The doors closed in front of me.

'My head's in a brain fuck, Mickey.'

'A brain fuck?'

'I've got Munchausen by proxy.'

Mickey was quiet on the phone. Everything that had seemed important wasn't anymore. The foundation on which I'd built myself didn't exist, it had become outmoded.

'I know you and Texas joke around and say that if a free dinner at Riche is being hosted on the same day as your funeral, regrettably I won't be attending the funeral.'

Mickey didn't comment.

'Mickey, I don't know how to do a fucking thing. I'm a hundred years old. At thirty-six I could still crack an egg into a bowl without getting any shell in it, but every omelette I've made in the last few years has had eggshells.'

'What are you talking about, Bibbs?'

'It's like it's all passed me by.'

People came down the platform, carrying plastic bags filled with water bottles and split watermelon, and they would compete to see who could spit the seeds the farthest, into the grass. I had no friends.

'I'm talking about what I said. . . About Baby. That it's not entirely true.'

Mickey gasped. We knew each other well, Mickey and I. Mickey had seen me. Not himself in me, but a chance to start over. A chance to transcend the real Mickey.

'Bibbs. Maybe you can't have it all.'

'It all? What do you mean?'

'Well, maybe you can't have the man and the career and the passion and everything. Maybe you have to choose.'

'But I don't have anything. . . none, of that?'

'Sure, that's true.'

Mickey was loving LA. That's why he wasn't about to argue. Another train was approaching, and I didn't get on that one either. I sat down on a bench and watched scantily clad people disappear. Today was going to be a crazy hot day.

A day this hot sparked madness. Today people would drown and betray each other, all because of the heat.

'At least you've made a choice, Bibbs. Lots of people don't.'

I squinted into the darkness of the tunnel, perhaps to see if another life was on its way.

'Yeah, that's true. At least I've made a choice.'

We hung up. I thought of Grandma. Ten years ago, we'd been so happy about my success. First you celebrate the small victories. A pair of shoes arrives in the mail and you've been working so damn hard and you might not have any shoes and the shoes seem to offer a community. You put them on. In the end, you have ten pairs of shoes in the hall that you feel nothing for. The days go by. Something about age that I couldn't articulate. OK, I thought, thinking of Nina. Be young. That too will pass.

A man who I noticed had recognised me had walked onto the platform. He was middle-aged and from a distance looked worse for wear, dressed far too warmly in suit trousers and a grey jacket.

'I recognise you,' he shouted, and I looked down at my vibrating phone. Baby was calling.

'Hoho,' said the man, who had come closer. I declined the call and looked up. To my surprise, I recognised him too.

'We met outside the casino!'

Right. His pockmarked skin. His poverty more obvious than it had been on Kungsgatan a few nights ago. A tooth was missing and always would be.

'Where are you going?'

The question shook me. I had no idea. Where were you going from Slipgatan if you weren't going back to Slipgatan? The man radiated kindness, like a dreamer, but I wanted to keep my guard up.

'Did you win anything that night?' I smiled, shaking my head as I let my gaze linger on the display counting down to the next train so that he would notice that he was bothering me. No, I hadn't won anything.

'You know what I always say,' the man said, taking a half-smoked cigarette out of his jacket pocket. Every nail rimmed with dirt and the sole of one loafer flapping.

'No, how am I supposed to know what you always say? We don't know each other.'

The man tilted his head.

'Sure we do.'

The mare attacked through a rift in the morning and I clutched my chest in surprise. The phone in my hand started vibrating again.

'Well, girl, I always say, "You haven't got a shot, so take one anyway!"'

I stared at the man, smiling so widely.

I stared at the screen, at Baby.

The man grabbed the cigarette without lighting it.

'Do you want to have breakfast together? It's on me! And then we can go do some gambling.'

I'm sorry, I said, but I have to take this. My face prickled like it was about to go numb, and I left the bench. The man batted away my apology.

'Nothing to apologise for. We'll have another chance, or not.'

I started walking towards the escalator and the man yelled after me. 'I think you and I will always have more chances!'

Baby sounded worried on the phone.

'Where did you go, Bibbs?'

I'm coming home now, darling. I ran into someone I knew, that's all. Baby said: I'll come meet you. Take the road along the water, and I could hear in his voice that he'd never let me go.

So, I passed through the barrier, up the stairs. The smell of piss hit me. The Italian restaurant on the corner hadn't opened and I sat down on the bench outside to choose an image. I chose one of Baby's hand over my breast, taken while we were sunbathing in the garden that happy summer.

'I want to thank you for all your support over the past few days,' I wrote under the picture and it felt easy.

Then I kept going. I wrote that Baby had decided to go to therapy and that he was going to get sober, all to make up for what he did to me. To become the man we both knew he could be. Baby was prepared to take responsibility for his actions and I was ready to forgive him. It wasn't conventional, I concluded, but when had I ever cared about convention.

'You've always supported me for being myself. I hope you will continue to do so in the future!' Without reading it over, I published the post, feeling light, in the flow. I was going to buy two EuroJackpot tickets and a scratchcard. This was the best I could do, for the money and Baby. For Slipgatan and for us. No, that wasn't true, but it could be. I went back into the app. Two people had commented, but I didn't bother reading. Instead, I looked carefully at the photo. The memory of us, tender in the garden, was vague, as if it were an event retold by someone else, a déjà vu from my own life. By night-fall, the sky would be filled with balloons. I had 100,000 kronor + my name. I had Baby.

Instead of walking up Långholmsgatan and taking Verk-stadsgatan home, I turned onto Bergsund Beach, as agreed. The first time I went into Marite's office she'd asked me what I needed help with and the question was more alien to me today than it had ever been. What help was there to be had? It's impossible to undo what has already been done. Of course I would have wished for the days to have unfolded differently. Of course I wished I had a stronger character. All of us weak characters have wished for that at some point. But wishing is easy. The hard part, and this I explained to Marite, is to bear the truth of one's life. Marite said she understood, but I wondered if she was being sincere.

On the other side of Liljeholmen Bay were those large con-crete buildings I knew nothing about, and I saw Baby emerge from the greenery, further down the street. Despite the crim-inal heat, he'd put on tight jeans and raised his hand in a wave when he saw me. I raised both hands in reply. Suddenly he stopped, shoved his hand into his pocket and took out his phone. He stopped to read what was on the screen. Someone had probably already got in touch about what I'd written. That's how interested they are in me. A bold heron was wheeling above the moored boats and the distance between me and Baby meant I couldn't tell by his pupils if the crazy switch had been flicked. I would find out in time. A jet ski roared past. It was summer and there was no smoke rising from the water. The sun was a fucking citrus cunt blazing in the sky.

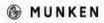 **MUNKEN**

Learn more about the paper we use:

www.arcticpaper.com

Arctic Paper UK Ltd
8 St Thomas Street
London
SE1 9RS